CUENTO
DE LUZ

A mis padres, a mis hijos, para Xabi… por vosotros escribí esta historia. Os quiero mucho.
— Paula Merlán

A mis padres, Nieves y Moisés, a mis hijos, Elías y Sabela, y a Ramiro.
Por todos vosotros haría cualquier cosa.
— Blanca Millán

PAPEL DE PIEDRA®
SIN ÁRBOLES · SIN AGUA · SIN CLORO

Este libro está impreso sobre **Papel de Piedra©** con el certificado de **Cradle to Cradle™** (plata). Cradle to Cradle™, que en español significa «de la cuna a la cuna», es una de las certificaciones ecológicas más rigurosa que existen y premia a aquellos productos que han sido concebidos y diseñados de forma ecológicamente inteligente.

Empresa
B
Certificada

Cuento de Luz™ se convirtió en 2015 en una **Empresa B Certificada©**. La prestigiosa certificación se otorga a empresas que utilizan el poder de los negocios para resolver problemas sociales y ambientales y cumplir con estándares más altos de desempeño social y ambiental, transparencia y responsabilidad.

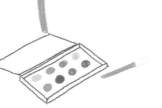

Por vosotros
© 2021 del texto: Paula Merlán
© 2021 de las ilustraciones: Blanca Millán
© 2021 Cuento de Luz SL
Calle Claveles, 10 | Urb. Monteclaro | Pozuelo de Alarcón | 28223 | Madrid | Spain
www.cuentodeluz.com
ISBN: 978-84-18302-08-4
1ª edición
Impreso en PRC por Shanghai Cheng Printing Company, enero 2021, tirada número 1826-4

POR VOSOTROS

Paula Merlán   Blanca Millán

Por vosotros haríamos cualquier cosa...

Comeríamos, sin rechistar, todas las verduras.

Cantaríamos, a dúo, bajo la lluvia.

Tejeríamos, con hilos alegres,
una manta infinita de besos.

Nos enfrentaríamos, con valentía,
a todos nuestros miedos.

Solucionaríamos, por arte de magia,
todas vuestras penas.

Dibujaríamos, con destreza, el camino hacia las estrellas...

Porque vosotros hacéis cualquier cosa por los dos.

Nos arropáis cuando hace frío.

Nos animáis a comenzar un nuevo camino.

Nos inspiráis, con entusiasmo, a superarnos.

Porque siempre estáis dispuestos a ayudarnos.

Nosotros haríamos cualquier cosa con tal de veros felices.

POR VOSOTROS

¡Muy felices!

¡Inmensamente felices!

Name_____ Date _____

Exploration and Settlement of Canada

The Norsemen, also known as the Vikings, were the first Europeans to land in what is now Canada. It is likely that the Norsemen, explorers from Norway and other Scandinavian countries, made contact with the Aboriginal peoples who were already living in what is now Canada. These men, with their leader, Leif Ericson, explored the coast of North America and called it Vinland. The Norsemen made their landing around the year 1000 A.D. This was almost five hundred years before Christopher Columbus was to discover America.

Around the year 1600, some 600 years after the Norsemen, explorers from England and France discovered Canada. These English and French explorers were trying to find a route called the Northwest Passage to reach the markets of China and India. They did not discover a shorter trading route to India. However, when they discovered Canada, they did find a land that had rich fishing resources and a large population of fur-bearing animals.

Jacques Cartier was a French explorer. In 1535, he explored the Gulf of St. Lawrence and claimed the land for France. In 1608, Samuel de Champlain, another Frenchman, established a colony at Quebec. He explored the region around Lake Huron and developed trading alliances with the Huron and Algonquin Indians in the area.

Henry Hudson, who was an Englishman, explored the area around Hudson Bay in 1610. The large bay he explored would later be named Hudson Bay. Through his explorations, Hudson claimed Canada for England.

Thus, the rival claims of England and France in Canada were established.

Refer to the map below and answer the questions that follow.

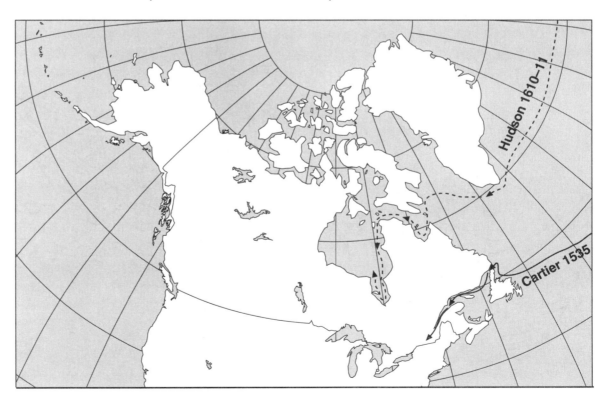

Name_____ Date _____

Use the map on page 1 to complete the activity below. Fill in the blanks with the terms listed below.

**England   France   Jacques Cartier   Henry Hudson
Samuel de Champlain   Leif Ericson**

1. Locate and label Hudson Bay on the map on page 1.

2. The English explorer who first explored this region was _____.

3. Locate and label the Gulf of St. Lawrence.

4. Locate and label the St. Lawrence River.

5. The European explorer who first explored the Gulf of St. Lawrence and the St. Lawrence River was _____.

6. Henry Hudson was an _____ explorer.

7. Jacques Cartier was a _____ explorer.

8. The Frenchman who settled Quebec and developed trading alliances with the Algonquin and Huron Indians was _____.

Name_____ Date _____

The French and English in Canada

The French who first came to Canada settled in the area that is now Quebec and the St. Lawrence Valley. The French called the area New France. The French were trappers and traders. Fur-bearing animals were plentiful, so the Frenchmen made a living by trapping the animals and sending the pelts back to France.

Refer to the map below to complete the following activity.

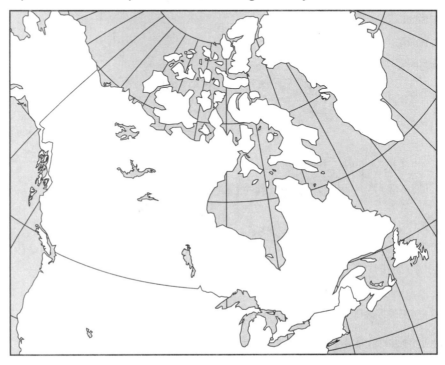

1. Locate and label the St. Lawrence River, Gulf of St. Lawrence, and Lake Huron.
2. Write the words "New France" from Lake Huron to the Gulf of St. Lawrence.
3. Write the words "French-controlled" alongside "New France."

While the French were building settlements in the area that is now Quebec, the English established the Hudson Bay Company in the Hudson Bay area of Canada. The Hudson Bay Company was formed by individuals in England who invested the money needed to establish a trading company.

For many years the English and French lived peacefully. Eventually, however, conflicts began to develop, which led to a major war.

4. Locate and label Hudson Bay on the map.
5. Write the words "English-controlled" in the area below the Hudson Bay.

Name_____ Date _____

Exploration Matching

Match each term in Column A with its definition in Column B.

Column A	Column B
_____ 6. Ericson	A. Name given to area controlled by France, including the St. Lawrence River Valley
_____ 7. Hudson	B. English explorer who claimed part of Canada for England
_____ 8. New France	C. Norseman who led Vikings in exploring the coast of North America
_____ 9. Hudson Bay	D. Famous bay in northern Canada
_____ 10. Champlain	E. French fortress in New France
_____ 11. Quebec	F. French explorer who claimed part of Canada for France

Canadian Time Line

Each of the statements below was a significant event in the early history of Canada. On the blanks below, rewrite the events, beginning with the one that occurred first and ending with the event that occurred last.

• Jacques Cartier explores Gulf of St. Lawrence and St. Lawrence River.

• Aboriginal peoples migrate to Canada from Asia.

• Lief Ericson explores Newfoundland and Atlantic Coast of Canada.

• Henry Hudson explores Hudson Bay region.

• Samuel de Champlain explores the St. Lawrence and Great Lakes.

1._____

2._____

3._____

4._____

5._____

Name_____ Date _____

Aboriginal Inhabitants of Canada

When Europeans arrived in Canada, they found a large Aboriginal population, that is, there were native people already living in Canada. Anthropologists believe the Aboriginal population came to Canada across the Bering Sea from Siberia. Many anthropologists believe the Aborigines came to Canada by crossing a land bridge between Siberia and North America over 30,000 years ago. The Aboriginal people lived by hunting, fishing, and farming. Today, the Aboriginal, or Indian, population includes over 500,000 people who make up over 600 bands.

The Europeans found that the Aboriginal people had learned to exist in an environment that was often very harsh. They had developed their own form of government. They also had rich traditions that were orally passed down from generation to generation.

Match each term in Column A with its definition in Column B.

Column A

_____ 1. Aboriginal population

_____ 2. Oral traditions

_____ 3. Europeans

_____ 4. Anthropologist

Column B

A. People from England, Spain, Portugal, and France who came to Canada

B. A person who studies customs, traditions, and origins of groups of people

C. Name given to the Indians who were living in Canada when the Europeans arrived

D. Refers to Aboriginal people telling younger generations about their culture

On Map 3 below, locate the following: Bering Sea, Bering Strait, Siberia.

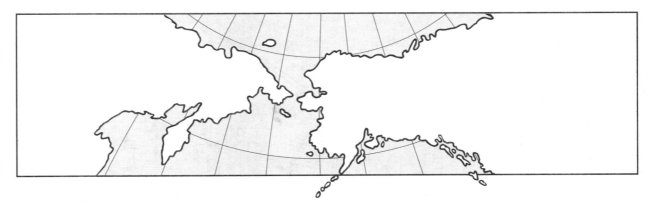

5. Siberia is part of which nation?   a) Canada   b) United States   c) Russia

6. The Bering Sea is between   a) North America and Asia   b) North America and Europe

   c) North America and Africa   d) North America and South America.

7. The Bering Sea is connected to the _____ Ocean by the _____ _____.

Name_____ Date _____

First Nations

       In Canada, the term "First Nations" is used to refer to the native Canadian Indians, or Aboriginal population. This term is used to remind Canadians that when the Europeans arrived, many of the Indian groups already had their own forms of government. The Canadian Indians, or "**First Nations**," are currently involved in **cultural**, **social**, **political**, and **economic** change.

       Complete the following blanks with the number of the phrase below that means the same as the words in bold in the above selection.

       In Canada, the term "First Nations" is used to refer to the Canadian Indians. This term is used to remind Canadians that when the Europeans arrived, many of the Indian groups already had their own forms of government. The Canadian Indians, or "_____," are currently involved in _____, _____, _____, and _____ change.

1. refers to the way a society lives and its traditions and beliefs

2. refers to the Indians living in Canada when the Europeans arrived

3. refers to government

4. refers to money, producing goods, and using or selling the goods produced

5. refers to living conditions, how people live, and health

Name_____ Date _____

Inuits, A First Nation

It is believed that the **Inuits**, or Eskimos, came to Canada across the Bering Strait during the last ice age. The Inuit live in the far north of Canada near the Arctic Circle. Although they lived in a harsh environment, the Inuit learned to thrive. Once in Canada, some of the Inuit settled near the coast and survived by hunting seal and walrus. This hunting could be very dangerous. The Inuit hunted by using a small boat called a **kayak**. Each kayak was manned by an individual who had to be very skillful and daring during the hunt.

While some Inuit settled near the coast, others chose to live in the far north, away from the coast. These Inuit hunted caribou and other land-dwelling animals. In the Inuit society, the family was very important. The survival of the Inuits both on the coast and inland was based on hunting. Several families made up a group that cooperated as a hunting party.

Read each of the following statements and place a plus (+) by the statement if it tells how the two Inuit groups are alike.

_____ 1. Both groups came to Canada across the Bering Strait.

_____ 2. Both groups used the kayak for hunting.

_____ 3. Both groups lived by hunting.

_____ 4. Both groups settled inland.

_____ 5. Both groups are part of a First Nation.

_____ 6. Both groups lived in a very harsh environment.

_____ 7. Both groups lived by hunting caribou.

_____ 8. In both groups, the family was very important.

Name_____ Date _____

Refer to Map 4 below and complete the activities. In the paragraphs on the previous page, it is stated that the Inuit live in the far northern parts of Canada. This activity will help you identify where the Inuit live in Canada.

1. Write the word **Inuit** at various locations around the Hudson Bay coast and along the coast of Labrador to locate where many of the coastal Inuits lived.

2. Write the word **Inuit** at various locations along the Arctic Circle. These locations indicate where many of the inland Inuits lived.

There is great change occurring today among the Inuit as they become part of the larger, highly industrialized society of Canada. Hunting and fishing are still important activities that provide food for the Inuit. However, seal hunting and fur trapping do not provide as much income as they once did. Today, the Inuit get an increased amount of their income by producing wood carvings and prints that reflect the Inuit culture. These items are sold in various parts of the world.

On April 1, 1999, the eastern part of the Northwest Territories, including Baffin Island, became **Nunavut Territory**. This new territory is largely the home of the Inuit and has the same political and economic rights as the other Canadian territories. Inuits will increasingly take an active role in the political and economic life of Canada. The western part of the Northwest Territories, also known as **Denendeh**, is a home for the ancient rivals of the Inuit, the **Dene**.

.me_____ Date _____

Inuit Crossword Puzzle

Use the clues below to complete the crossword puzzle about the Inuit. Refer to the Inuit information on pages 6 through 8 to find the answers.

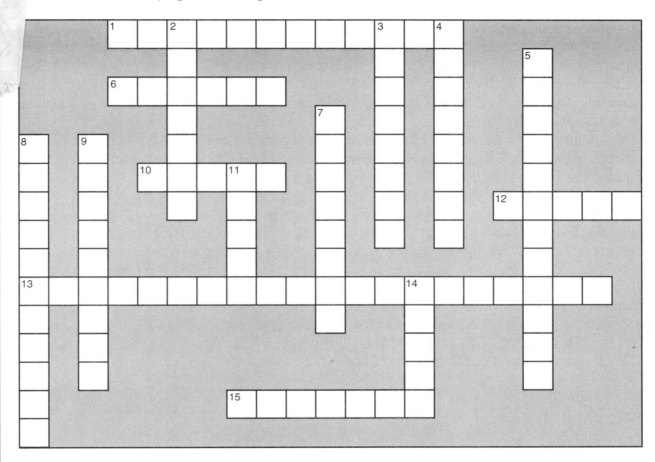

ACROSS

1. The Inuit live in the far north near the _____ _____.
6. Name of the strait across which the Inuit migrated to Canada
10. Some Inuit settled near the _____ and hunted sea animals.
12. Boat used to hunt seal and walrus.
13. One of the territories in Canada (two words)
15. Name given to the new Inuit territory carved from the Northwest Territories

DOWN

2. Animal hunted by the inland Inuit
3. Word that refers to beliefs, customs, and traditions of the Inuit
4. Word that refers to a change in how the Inuit make a living
5. Items produced by the Inuit and sold around the world (two words)
7. Home of the Dene, the rivals of the Inuit
8. Term that refers to the Aboriginal people of Canada (two words)
9. What Inuit families must do to survive
11. Animals hunted by coastal Inuit
14. Name given to one of the First Nation groups

Name_____ Date _____

War Develops Between France and England

     Soon a conflict developed between the French and English, as each group tried to gain greater control of Canada and the trade with the Indians, including the fur trade. Although fur-bearing animals were plentiful, the French and English became enemies, and this encouraged each country's Indian allies to become enemies, as well.

     Conflicts between France and England over trade with the Indians and the fur trade became more frequent. Finally, in 1756, the French and English became engaged in a war that lasted until 1763. It was known as the "French and Indian" War because the French and some Indian tribes, mainly the Huron and Algonquin, were allied against the British and their Indian allies, the Iroquois.

     Many battles were fought, but one of the most important was the battle for the French fortress at Quebec. This fortress was the most important French settlement in New France. Finally, the British won the battle and conquered the fortress. The loss of the fortress was a fatal blow to the French in Canada.

     In 1763, the war ended and the Treaty of Paris was signed. This treaty gave England all of the French territory in North America east of the Mississippi River except for the city of New Orleans. Once the treaty was signed, Canada became a British colony.

     Even though France withdrew from Canada, thousands of Frenchmen remained in Canada to live. Although Canada was now a British colony, the Frenchmen who remained continued to speak French and follow French customs and traditions. In 1774, Britain passed the Quebec Act, which officially recognized French civil laws and the French language in Quebec. The influence of the French is still dominant in Quebec, where the French language and customs are still spoken and followed.

     Complete the blanks in the following selection. Use words from the list below to complete the blanks.

French	**Quebec**	**English**	**British colony**	**1763**
French and Indian		**Treaty of Paris**	**Quebec Act**	**1756**
New France				

     Canada became a (1)_____ _____ in the year (2)_____ , when the (3) _____ of _____ was signed. This treaty ended the (4) _____ _____ _____ War. This Treaty of Paris gave all of the (5)_____ territory east of the Mississippi to the English.

     The fortress at (6)_____ was an important French settlement. The area in the St. Lawrence River Valley where large numbers of Frenchmen lived was known as (7)_____ _____.

     In 1774, the (8)_____ _____ officially recognized the French language, customs, and traditions for those who lived in Quebec.

Name_____ Date _____

Canada Becomes Home to the Loyalists

The history of the British colony in Canada was to develop far differently from the history of the 13 colonies that would one day become the United States. The Canadian colony remained loyal to the British government, while the 13 American colonies in 1776 rebelled and won their independence. The 13 colonies became the United States, an independent nation. Canada chose to remain a colony of Great Britain.

Many people living in the 13 colonies did not agree with the war against the British. These people were called **loyalists**. The loyalists wanted to remain a part of the British Empire and not become independent. When the 13 colonies gained their independence, many of these loyalists left the newly formed United States and went to Canada. Large numbers of the loyalists who left the United States settled in the colonies of Nova Scotia and New Brunswick.

Refer to the map below and complete the following activity.

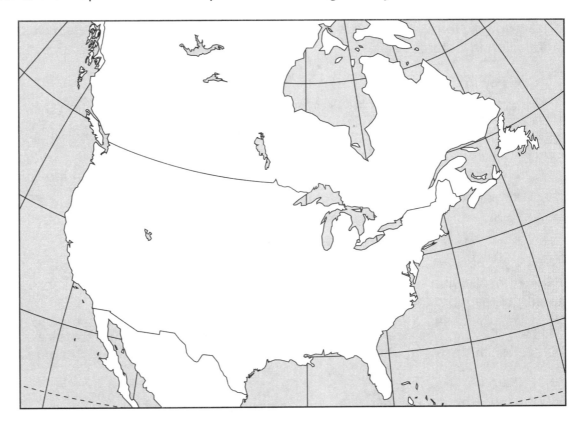

1. Color the area where the 13 colonies are located. These colonies became independent from Great Britain and became the United States.
2. Locate the colonies of Nova Scotia and New Brunswick on the map. Color the area where they are located on the map.
3. Draw a series of arrows from the 13 colonies to Nova Scotia and New Brunswick. Write the words "Loyalists move to Canada" along the arrows.

Name_____ Date _____

Canada Becomes a Constitutional Monarchy

By the year 1867, the British colonies in Canada included Lower Canada (Quebec), Upper Canada (Ontario), Nova Scotia, and New Brunswick. Each of these colonies was an independent colony. Many in Canada were fearful that the United States was becoming powerful and might annex the Canadian colonies. In an effort to become stronger, these four independent Canadian colonies joined together and became the **Dominion of Canada**. Even though they had joined together and formed one colony, they still remained a part of the British Empire.

The government that was established to govern the Dominion of Canada was based on the British Parliamentary system. The Parliament was composed of a House of Commons and Senate. However, the British still had a representative in Canada called the governor general. The Dominion of Canada had a great deal of autonomy, but it was still part of the British Empire. Canadians still felt a great allegiance to the king or queen of England.

The following terms are used in the above selection. Match each term in Column A with its definition in Column B.

Column A	Column B
_____ 1. Independent	A. Refers to loyalty of Canadians to British Crown
_____ 2. Annex	B. Refers to the fear that the United States might add Canada to the U.S.
_____ 3. Dominion	C. Title used by self-governing nations in the British Commonwealth
_____ 4. Autonomy	D. Refers to self-government
_____ 5. Allegiance	E. Refers to freedom from control of others

Read the following selection and write the letter of the word or phrase that agrees with the meaning of the word the blank follows.

A. free   **B. add**   **C. loyalty to the British Empire**
D. freedom to run government   **E. self-government, but still part of the British Empire**

By the year 1867, the British colonies in Canada included Upper and Lower Canada, Nova Scotia, and New Brunswick. Each of these was a British colony **independent** (6)_____ from the other colonies. Many in Canada were fearful that the United States was becoming powerful and might **annex** (7)_____ the Canadian colonies.

The government that was established to govern the **Dominion** (8)_____ of Canada was based on the British Parliamentary system. The Dominion of Canada had a great deal of **autonomy** (9)_____, but it was still part of the British Empire. Canadians still had a great **allegiance** (10)_____ to the king or queen of England.

Canadian Expansion

After 1867, Canada began to expand westward. In the northwest was the large area around Hudson Bay that belonged to the Hudson Bay Company. The company also owned land in the interior of Canada. The Hudson Bay Company was owned by a large group of English citizens who had been granted this land by King Charles of England. The urge to expand made it desirable that the land owned by the Hudson Bay Company become part of Canada. This was accomplished when the area, known as Rupert's Land, was purchased by the Dominion of Canada from the English owners. This middle west later became the provinces of Alberta, Manitoba, and Saskatchewan, and it makes up part of the Northwest Territories.

In 1870, the province of Manitoba was added to the Dominion of Canada. Then, in 1871, the crown colony British Columbia decided to become part of the Dominion of Canada. Prince Edward Island joined in 1873, and in 1898, the Yukon Territory was established. Two new provinces, Alberta and Saskatchewan, were added in 1905. Finally, in 1949, the last British Colony, Newfoundland, became a Canadian province.

Residents of the Northwest Territories voted in 1992 to divide the territories along an east-west boundary line. The eastern territory was named Nunavut, an Inuit word meaning "our land." It became a territory on April 1, 1999.

Canada and the United States Expand Westward

After the United States gained its independence from Great Britain, it began to expand. Canada was expanding at the same time.

The following table shows the dates when provinces or territories were added as Canada and the United States expanded westward. However, the events are not in the proper order. Create a time line for the westward expansion of Canada by placing the events in chronological order on the next page.

Canada Expands Westward

1870 Purchases Hudson Bay and Rupert's Land area
1873 Prince Edward Island becomes province
1898 Yukon Territory established
1905 Alberta becomes province
1867 Dominion of Canada
      (Ontario, Quebec, Nova Scotia, New Brunswick)
1905 Saskatchewan becomes province
1870 Manitoba becomes province
1949 Newfoundland becomes province
1999 Nunavut becomes a territory
1870 Northwest Territories established
1871 British Columbia becomes province

Name_____ Date _____

1. Place each of the dates and events on the time line below to show the expansion of Canada.

|——|
1867   1999

The United States Expands Westward

1848 Mexican Cession (Includes: CA, UT, CO, NM, AZ)

1783 Original territory gained from England in Revolutionary War (Includes: NH, MA, RI, CT, NY, PA, NJ, DE, MD, VA, NC, SC, GA, VT, ME, OH, IN, MI, WI, IL, KY, TN, AL, MS, WV)

1853 Gadsden Purchase (Includes parts of NM and AZ)

1819 Florida annexed (Includes FL and parts of AL, MS, and LA)

1846 Oregon Country annexed (Includes OR, WA, and ID)

1867 Alaska purchased

1898 Hawaii annexed

1803 Louisiana Purchase (Includes: LA, AR, MO, IA, MN, ND, SD, MT, NE, KA, OK, and WY)

1845 Texas annexed (Includes TX and parts of NM, OK, CO, and WY)

2. Place each of the dates and events on the time line below to show the expansion of the United States.

|——|
1783   1898

Name_____ Date _____

3. Imagine you are a Canadian citizen in 1803. The United States purchases the Louisiana Territory and more than doubles its size. U.S. citizens begin to move westward in large numbers. The nation is obviously feeling the need to expand. There are rumors that some in the United States are thinking that Canada should be part of the United States. Write what your thoughts, concerns, or feelings might be about this U.S. expansion and the rumors you are hearing.

_____

_____

_____

_____

_____

_____

_____

4. Imagine you are the same Canadian citizen as in the previous exercise. It is the year 1846, and the United States has just won a war with Mexico, and now Texas and what will one day become Arizona, California, Colorado, New Mexico, and Utah are part of the United States. You hear that the United States and Great Britain have a disagreement over the Oregon Country. Find out where the Oregon Country is located. Write what your thoughts, concerns, or feelings might be about the U.S. expansion and the rumors you are hearing. What will you be suggesting to your Canadian friends?

_____

_____

_____

_____

_____

_____

_____

Name_____ Date _____

Refer to the map below and the one on the next page to complete the following activities.

5. Color in the states in the United States to show westward expansion. Use a different color for each major section that was added to the country. Label each state and indicate the date it was admitted to the Union as a state. (Refer to an American history textbook, encyclopedia, almanac, or some other source to determine the date of admission.)

Name_____ Date _____

6. Color in the provinces in Canada to show westward expansion. Use a different color for each major section that was added to the country. Label each province and indicate the date it was admitted as a province.

Name_____ Date _____

Canada Becomes an Independent Nation

Canada maintained a Dominion status until 1931. In 1931, the Statute of Westminster was passed by Great Britain. This statute made Canada autonomous. However, Canadians still wanted to have an association with the British Empire. To maintain this association, a governor-general appointed by the King or Queen represents the Royal Throne in Canada. However, the governor-general is only a figurehead and has no power to determine how Canada is governed. All of the decisions about how Canada is governed now belong to the Canadians.

Answer the following questions.

1. The United States became independent from Great Britain in 1776. The United States has been an independent nation for _____ years.

2. Canada has been an independent nation for _____ years.

3. Which phrase best defines the term "figurehead"?

      (a) great authority   (b) no authority

4. Draw the flag of Canada in the space below. Refer to an encyclopedia or other source, if necessary.

Name_____ Date _____

Canada's Government

Canada has a **federal** system of government. This means that the power to govern is divided between the national government and the governments in the provinces. The national government has specific governing authority, and the provinces have specific governing authority.

The government of Canada functions much like the government of Great Britain. It is a **parliamentary** type of government. The parliament makes the laws and carries them out. The Canadian Parliament has a Senate and House of Commons. Members of the House of Commons are elected. Elections are held at least every five years, but they may be held whenever the majority party is voted down or calls an election. The members of the Senate are appointed and may serve until age 75.

In Canada, there are political parties that represent the people in the Senate and House of Commons. The major political parties are: the Liberal party, the Progressive Conservatives, and the New Democratic party. The leader of the government is the **prime minister**. The prime minister is elected by the party in control of the parliament. Once elected, the prime minister chooses a **cabinet**. The cabinet members are appointed to specific jobs in the government.

Fill in the following rectangles to show the structure of the Canadian national government. Use the terms below to complete the rectangles.

Elects Prime Minister   **Senate**   **House of Commons**   **Appointed**
Elected   **Appoints Cabinet**   **Parliament**

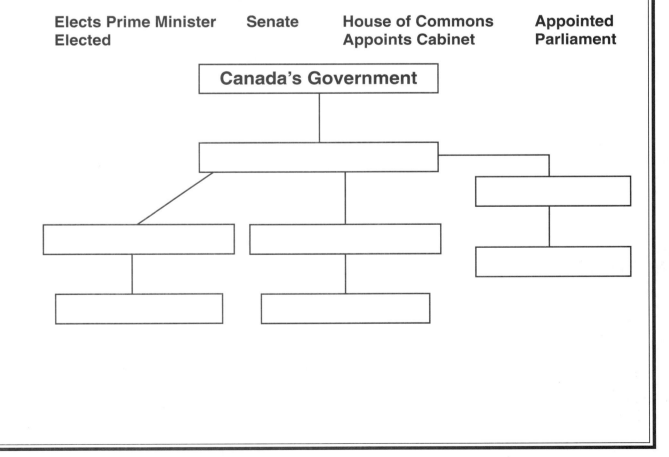

Name_____ Date _____

The United States Government

     Like Canada, the United States has a **federal** system of government. The powers of government are divided between the national and state governments. In the United States, the legislative branch of the government is the Congress. The Congress makes laws but does not enforce the laws. Congress is made up of the Senate and House of Representatives. The members of the Senate are elected by the people for a term of six years. The members of the House of Representatives are elected by the people for a term of two years. Unlike Canada, elections cannot be called at any time. Elections for the president, senators, and representatives occur at the end of a set number of years.

     The leader of the United States government is the **president**. The president is elected by the people for a term of four years. After the people elect the president, the president appoints a cabinet that is confirmed by the Senate.

U.S. Cabinet Offices

State	Housing and Urban Development
Treasury	Labor
Defense	Health and Human Services
Justice	Transportation
Interior	Energy
Agriculture	Education
Commerce	Veterans Affairs

Use the terms below to complete the blanks in the following selection.

Congress	**House of Representatives**	**president**	**four**
federal	**Senate**	**state**	**two**
legislative	**Cabinet**	**six**	**national**

     The government of the United States is a (1)_____ system. The (2)_____ makes the laws but does not carry out the laws. The Congress includes the (3)_____ and (4)_____ of _____. Senators are elected for a term of (5)_____ years. The members of the House of Representatives are elected for a term of (6)_____years.

     The leader of the government is the (7)_____, who is elected by the people for a term of (8)_____ years. The (9)_____ is chosen by the president and confirmed by the (10)_____ .

     The system of government in the United States is a (11)_____ system. In a federal system, the power to govern is divided between the (12)_____ government and the (13)_____ governments.

Name_____ Date _____

14. In the space below, compare and contrast the governments of the United States and Canada. (Compare how the president and prime minister are selected for their offices, how the Congress and Parliament members are selected, how long the president, prime minister, members of Congress, and members of Parliament are in office, and so on. Compare the makeup of the Canadian cabinet to the U.S. cabinet.) You may need to use history books, encyclopedias, almanacs, and other sources to find information about the Canadian and U.S. governments. Continue on your own paper if necessary.

_____

_____

_____

_____

_____

_____

_____

15. You have learned that the governments of Canada and the United States are both alike and different. The terms below refer to the governments of Canada and the United States. Rectangle A is for terms that belong with Canada only. Rectangle B is for terms that belong with the United States only. Rectangle C is for terms that belong with both Canada and the United States. Place the number for each of the terms in Rectangle A, B, or C.

1. Prime Minister   7. Parliament
2. Senators elected by people   8. People elect president
3. Congress   9. Prime Minister appointed
4. House of Representatives   10. House of Commons
5. President   11. Federal government
6. Senate   12. Senators appointed

A	B	C

Name _____ Date _____

Canada: A Nation of Many Cultures

People from all over the world have immigrated to Canada and the United States. These immigrants, along with the native Americans, make both nations unique among the nations of the world.

France and the British Isles have contributed more to the population than any other groups. However, Canada is a multicultural society with large numbers of citizens of German, Italian, Ukrainian, Dutch, Polish, Chinese, Southeast Asian, Caribbean, Portuguese, and Scandinavian heritages.

In Canada, immigrants from certain countries have often settled in certain provinces. For example, large numbers of French are found in Quebec. In New Brunswick, Nova Scotia, and Cape Breton Island one finds large numbers of people whose lineage goes back to the British Isles.

Refer to the map below. Locate the Gaspe Peninsula, Nova Scotia, New Brunswick, Cape Breton Island, and Quebec.

Nova Scotia

When present-day Nova Scotia was settled in the early 1600s, it was known as New Scotland. King James of Scotland encouraged the settlement of New Scotland by granting the title "Baronet of Nova Scotia" to Scottish settlers who would purchase land in New Scotland and move there from Scotland.

In the 1620s, settlers arrived at New Scotland from Scotland and began settling the land. Within three years of their arrival, however, the colony came under the control of the French. When the French gained control, the Scottish settlers were required to leave New Scotland and return to Scotland.

New Scotland was now settled by Frenchmen. Under the French, the region was called Acadia and those settling there were called French Acadians. Acadia was a French settlement of primarily farmers. Soon the region was a land of prosperous farming and fishing communities. The language, religion, and the entire culture was French.

For the next 100 years after the French gained control of New Scotland, the conflict between the English and French continued. Finally, in 1713, the English regained control of Acadia, and the Scottish immigrants began returning to New Scotland.

The English gave the French Acadians the option of staying in Nova Scotia if they would agree to certain conditions. However, in 1775, the French Acadians were expelled from Nova Scotia. After the French Acadians were expelled, many of the new settlers in Nova Scotia came from the New England colonies in America.

Today, Nova Scotia is an example of the rich cultures that are found in the Canadian nation. The influence of both the French and Scottish are still evident.

The French Acadians Leave Nova Scotia

Although the British gave the Acadians the option of staying on their land when they gained control of Acadia (Nova Scotia), there was much conflict between the Acadians and the British. Finally, in 1775, the British drove the Frenchmen out of Acadia and took control of the land and livestock. The Acadians departed from Canada. Some went to the English colonies in America, others to the Caribbean Islands, and some returned to France. A group of the Acadians settled in the bayou country of Louisiana. The bayou country is a very swampy area near the mouth of the Mississippi River. Here they were known as Cajuns.

When the Acadians arrived in Louisiana, it was owned by Spain, but in 1803 it became a French possession again. Only a few weeks after the French gained control of Louisiana from the Spanish, however, President Thomas Jefferson authorized the purchase of Louisiana by the United States. The area purchased was known as the Louisiana Territory, and it included the bayou area settled by the Acadians.

The Cajun culture is recognized as a very rich culture. It has contributed much to the American way of life. The Cajuns are known for their unique food and music. However, many descendants of the original Cajuns have made important contributions in other areas, including education and politics.

Name_____ Date _____

Refer to the map below and complete the following activity.

1. Locate and label Nova Scotia on the map.
2. The area labeled with the symbol (/////) is the bayou country of Louisiana. Color in this area.

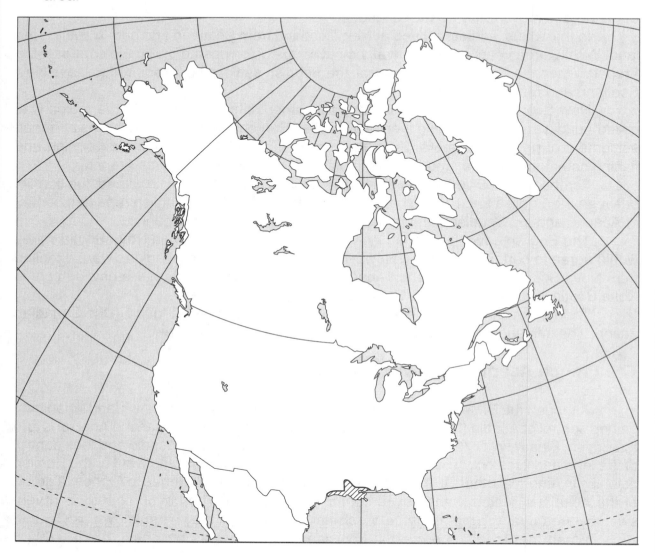

When the Acadians were forced to leave Canada, they went to many different parts of the world. However, many came to the English colonies of Virginia, Pennsylvania, Maryland, Georgia, North Carolina, and South Carolina. Later, many left those colonies to settle in Louisiana near the mouth of the Mississippi River.

3. Locate each of the following colonies on the map above by placing the letter on the map in the area where the colony was located.

    a) Virginia   b) Pennsylvania   c) Maryland
    d) Georgia   e) North Carolina   f) South Carolina

Name _____ Date _____

The French Acadians in Longfellow's "Evangeline"

One group of Acadians settled in the English colony of Maryland. There a man known by the name of Louis Arceneaux and a young lady named Emmeline Labiche met the poet Henry Wadsworth Longfellow. Longfellow wrote a story about the Acadians titled "Evangeline." Louis Arceneaux became Gabriel in Longfellow's "Evangeline," and Emmeline Labiche inspired Evangeline in the story.

In "Evangeline," Longfellow describes the peaceful and prosperous life of the Acadians in Nova Scotia before they were expelled by the English. Evangeline is a beautiful girl with many suitors who is living an idyllic life in Acadia. Gabriel, the son of a blacksmith, was Evangeline's preferred suitor. Together they were happy in the company of each other as they grew from childhood to adulthood in Acadia.

Longfellow describes the coming of the English ships and the command that all Acadians must meet in the church and hear His Majesty's mandate. Longfellow describes the pomp and ceremony as His Majesty's commander approaches the church and delivers the message that the land, livestock, and most possessions of the Acadians must be forfeited to the crown and that the Acadians will be banished from Acadia.

The exiled French Acadians then leave for various parts of the world. Gabriel and Evangeline are separated. Evangeline goes to the English colonies. Over the years she wanders from place to place trying to find Gabriel. Often she would find an individual who would say, "Oh yes! Gabriel is a Voyageur in the lowlands of Louisiana." Finally, Evangeline and a contingent of Acadians decide to travel by boat down the Ohio River to the Mississippi River and on to Louisiana. Longfellow describes the long trip down the rivers to the bayou country of Louisiana.

1. On the blanks below, write an ending for "Evangeline" as you think it might have happened. Then find a copy of "Evangeline" and see how close your ending is to the one written by Longfellow.

_____

_____

_____

_____

_____

_____

_____

_____

_____

Name_____ Date _____

2. The terms in Column A appear in the above selection describing "Evangeline." Column B has the meanings for the terms in Column A. Match the meaning with the term, by placing the letter from Column B on the line next to the corresponding term in Column A.

Column A

_____ Expelled
_____ Idyllic
_____ Mandate
_____ Pomp
_____ Voyageur
_____ Contingent
_____ Suitor
_____ Forfeited
_____ Majesty
_____ Exiled

Column B

A. Group going with Evangeline
B. Forced out or sent away by an authority
C. Ostentatious or vain display
D. A man who courts a woman
E. Title used when referring to a king or queen
F. To be forced to live away from one's country or community
G. Simple and charming way of life
H. A boatman who transported goods and men to trading posts
I. An authoritative order or command
J. Given up as a fine or penalty

3. On the blanks below, tell how Longfellow describes Evangeline.

_____

_____

_____

_____

_____

_____

_____

4. On the blanks below, tell how Longfellow describes Gabriel.

_____

_____

_____

_____

_____

_____

Name _____ Date _____

The Atlantic Provinces

Today the provinces of Newfoundland, Prince Edward Island, Nova Scotia, and New Brunswick are known as the Atlantic Provinces. Locate the provinces on a map and answer the following questions.

1. The province of _____ _____ _____ is an island.

2. The provinces of _____ _____ and _____ _____ are peninsulas.

3. The province of _____ contains a large island and territory on the mainland.

4. St. John's is the capital of _____ province.

5. Halifax is the capital of _____ _____ province.

6. Charlottetown is the capital of _____ _____ _____ province.

7. Fredericton is the capital of _____ _____ province.

8. The Bay of Fundy is located between:

    a) Newfoundland and New Brunswick.

    b) Nova Scotia and New Brunswick.

    c) Nova Scotia and Prince Edward Island.

Name _____ Date _____

The Unique Bay of Fundy

The Bay of Fundy has the world's record for high and low tides that occur each 24-hour period. When the tide is low, the boats in the harbor are all on dry ground. When high tide comes in, the same boats are floating up to 70 feet above the ground they were resting on at low tide.

The Bay of Fundy is very narrow. Because the Bay is so narrow, it causes the high tide to come in very rapidly. The tide comes in as a huge wall of water called a **tidal bore**.

Why does high tide and low tide occur twice every 24 hours? To explore this question, we will refer to the diagram below and answer the questions that follow.

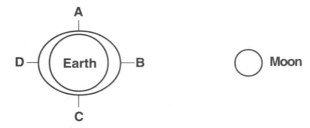

1. The oval surrounding the earth in the diagram above represents the oceans of the world. Color the area inside the oval blue.

2. High tide occurs when the moon is directly overhead at a given location on the earth. When high tide occurs, the water bulges   a) away from   b) toward   the moon.

3. In the above diagram, the water bulges toward the moon at point   a) D   b) B   c) C   d) A.

4. In the above diagram, high tide is also occurring at point   a) D   b) B   c) C   d) A.

5. In the above diagram, low tide is occurring at two points. The points where low tide is occurring are   a) A/D   b) B/D   c) C/B   d) A/C.

6. Write "high" by the letters where high tide is occurring.

7. Write "low" by the letters where low tide is occurring.

8. High tide would occur   a) 1   b) 2   c) 3   d) 4   time(s) each 24 hours.

9. Low tide would occur   a) 1   b) 2   c) 3   d) 4   time(s) each 24 hours.

10. High tide will occur again at "B" when the moon is directly overhead at   a) A   b) C   c) D.

11. Low tide will occur at "B" when the moon is directly overhead at   a) A/C   b) C/D   c) A/D.

Name _____ Date _____

12. In the previous diagram, high tide is occurring on the side facing the moon. High tide

    occurs because of the gravitational attraction of the _____.

13. In the previous diagram you can see that high tide is occurring on the side of the earth

    closest to the moon. However, high tide is also occurring on the opposite side of the

    earth away from the moon. In the space below, write a possible explanation for the high

    tide that occurs on the opposite side of the earth away from the moon.

    _____

    _____

    _____

    _____

    _____

14. The earth makes a complete revolution on its axis once every 24 hours. The people

    living near the Bay of Fundy would experience high tide   a) 1   b) 2   c) 3   d) 4   time(s)

    in a 24-hour period.

15. The people living near the Bay of Fundy would experience low tide   a) 1   b) 2

    c) 3   d) 4   time(s) in a 24-hour period.

Name _____ Date _____

Quebec

Over one-fourth of Canadians are French Canadians. The French Canadians are descendants of the French colonists who came to Canada during the 1500s and 1600s. Most French Canadians live in the province of Quebec.

The influence of the customs brought from France are very strong in Quebec. In Quebec, French is the most common language spoken. Streets and parks have French names, and most signs are written in French. In Canada, as a nation, 75 percent of the people speak English and 25 percent speak French. In Quebec, however, 80 percent of the people speak French and only 20 percent speak English.

Canada is a **bilingual** country. French and English are the two official languages. Canadian money is printed in French and English. The government conducts business in both French and English. Many businesses and government offices answer the phone in English and French.

Refer to the map below and complete the following activity. This activity will show that Canada is a nation with citizens whose heritage represents many parts of the world.

1. Draw a line from France to the area of Quebec Province in Canada.
2. Circle Great Britain and Ireland. Draw a line from these nations to Nova Scotia, Ontario, and New Brunswick Provinces in Canada.

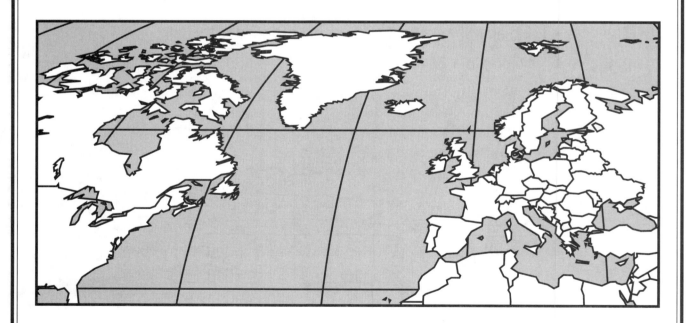

Name _____ Date _____

Canada's Population

Population Growth

Today it is important for a nation to determine how much the population will increase. Nations use the information about population growth to make plans for the future.

The example below shows how to project population increases and the total number of people a nation will have in future years.

Example: **Present population X rate of growth = increase in population for a year**. Then add the increase in population to the present population to get the total population at the end of the year.

In 1998, Canada's population is approximately 30,000,000. The annual population is increasing at a rate of 1.0 percent. To perform the mathematics, 1.0 percent must be converted to the decimal form before multiplying. To change the percent to a decimal, move the decimal point two places to the left and drop the percent sign. Example: 1.0% = 0.01 decimal form.

Formula to determine Canada's population in 1999:

30,000,000 X 0.01 = 300,000

The population in 1999 will be 300,000 greater than in 1998.

Add the increase to the current population.

30,000,000 + 300,000 = 30,300,000

The population in 1999 will be 30,300,000.

Complete the following table to project Canada's population growth for the 10-year period. Assume the 1.0 percent population increase remains stable for the 10-year period. The first year has been completed for you.

Table I

Year	Population	Percent Increase	Projected Population
1998	30,000,000	1.0%	30,300,000
1999	30,300,000	1.0%	
2000			
2001			
2002			
2003			
2004			
2005			
2006			
2007			

Name_____ Date _____

Comparing Canada to Other Nations of the World

Area

Listed below are the 10 largest nations in the world in area. Use the blanks on the right and rank the countries in size from "1," the largest, to "10," the smallest.

Country	Area in Square Miles	Countries Ranked
United States	3,618,765	1. _____
Canada	3,851,788	2. _____
Brazil	3,286,472	3. _____
China	3,705,386	4. _____
Australia	2,967,893	5. _____
Russia	6,592,800	6. _____
Kazakstan	1,049,150	7. _____
India	1,269,338	8. _____
Algeria	919,590	9. _____
Argentina	1,068,296	10. _____

Complete Graph I below to compare the areas of the above countries. Your teacher will explain how to make a bar or line graph.

Graph I: The Ten Largest Countries in Area

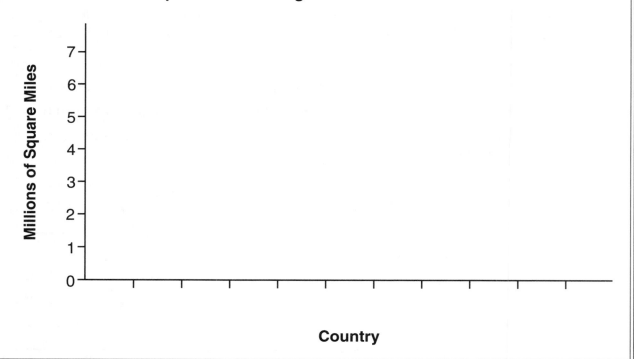

Name _____ Date _____

Population

Listed below are the 10 largest countries in the world in terms of population. Use the blanks on the right and rank the countries in population size from "1," the largest, to "10," the smallest. Answer the questions that follow.

Country	Population		Countries Ranked
United States	263,563,000	1.	_____
Brazil	161,416,000	2.	_____
China	1,226,944,000	3.	_____
Mexico	93,342,000	4.	_____
Indonesia	198,644,000	5.	_____
India	942,989,000	6.	_____
Bangladesh	118,342,000	7.	_____
Pakistan	143,595,000	8.	_____
Japan	125,156,000	9.	_____
Russia	148,385,000	10.	_____

The population of Canada is 29,972,000.

Complete Graph II below to compare the size of the populations in the above countries. Your teacher will explain how to make a bar or line graph.

Graph II: The Ten Largest Countries in Population

Population in Millions

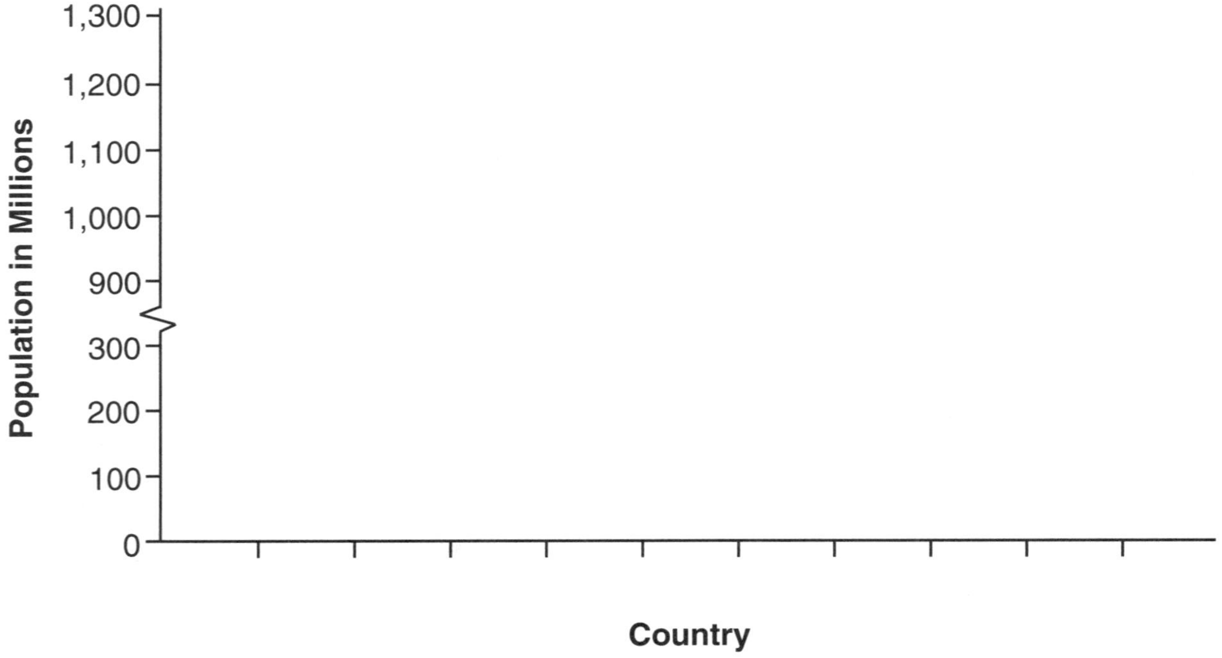

1,300 —
1,200 —
1,100 —
1,000 —
900 —
300 —
200 —
100 —
0 —

Country

Name _____ Date _____

Finding the Number of Persons Per Square Mile (Population Density)

      To find the number of persons per square mile (also called the **population density**), the population of the nation must be divided by the area of the nation.

      For example, suppose we wanted to find the population density of the nation of Forgotonia. The area of Forgotonia is 1,000 square miles. The population of Forgotonia is 10,000 persons.

10,000 (population) divided by 1,000 (area) = 10 persons per square mile.
Formula: **population/area = persons per square mile**.
10,000/1,000 = 10

      Let's take a real-life example now. Japan has an area of 145,869 square miles. The population of Japan is 125,156,000.

125,156,000/145,869 = 858

The number of persons per square mile in Japan is 858.

      In the following activity, you must determine the number of persons per square mile for Canada, the United States, China, India, Russia, and Brazil. Round all answers to the nearest whole number. (Use the information on pages 32 and 33).

1. There are approximately _____ people per square mile in Russia.

2. There are approximately _____ people per square mile in China.

3. There are approximately _____ people per square mile in Brazil.

4. There are approximately _____ people per square mile in the United States.

5. There are approximately _____ people per square mile in India.

6. There are approximately _____ people per square mile in Canada.

Name _____ Date _____

Finding the Ratio of Canadians to Other Nations of the World

How many people live in Canada compared to the United States, China, India, or Brazil? Another way of saying this is, "What is the ratio of persons in Canada to the United States?". A ratio is a number like 4:1, 4 to 1, or 4/1.

For example, let's say there are two countries called Gondland and Forttonia. Gondland has 6,000 people. Forttonia has 600 people. Divide 6,000 by 600 and you find there are 10 people in Gondland for every one person in Forttonia.

$$6,000 \div 600 = 10$$

Here is another example. Japan has a population of 125,156,000, and Mexico has a population of 93,342,000. What is the ratio of people in Japan to people in Mexico?

$$125,156,000 \div 93,342,000 = 1.3$$

There are 1.3 people in Japan for every one person in Mexico or 1.3/1.

Answer the following. Round to the nearest whole number, since you cannot have part of a person. (Use the information from page 33).

1. There are a)_____ persons in Russia for each person in Canada.

The ratio is b)_____/_____ .

2. There are a)_____ persons in Brazil for each person in Canada.

The ratio is b)_____/_____ .

3. There are a)_____ persons in the United States for each person in Canada.

The ratio is b)_____/_____ .

4. There are a)_____ persons in India for each person in Canada.

The ratio is b)_____/_____ .

5. There are a)_____ persons in China for each person in Canada.

The ratio is b)_____/_____ .

Name _____ Date _____

Where Canada's Population Lives

The population of Canada is not evenly distributed across this large nation. In fact, most of the people live on a very small part of the total territory of Canada. Refer to the map on page 37 and complete the activity below.

1. Color inside the dashed lines on the map to show where most of the people of Canada live.

2. Place dots on the map to locate the cities of Vancouver, Calgary, Edmonton, Winnipeg, London, Hamilton, Toronto, Ottawa, and Montreal. These are cities where a large number of people live. The number of people per square mile is often over 250 in these cities.

3. Refer back to page 34 and find the average number of persons per square mile for all of Canada.

4. Most of the people of Canada live:

    a) spread out across Canada.

    b) in a narrow band across southern Canada near the U.S. border.

    c) along the shores of Hudson Bay.

5. Place a plus (+) by any of the statements below that you think might be a reason why most Canadians live near the southern border of Canada.

_____ a) Large areas of northern Canada have a long, cold winter.

_____ b) Large areas of northern Canada have a very short growing season.

_____ c) Large areas of northern Canada are located in the polar region.

_____ d) The climate near the southern border is milder than in the north.

_____ e) The most fertile soils are found in southern Canada.

_____ f) The growing season for crops is longer in southern Canada.

_____ g) The Great Lakes and the St. Lawrence River are important transportation routes.

_____ h) Large areas of northern Canada have very poor soils.

Name _____ Date _____

Population of Canada Map

Name _____ Date _____

Political Regions: Provinces and Territories

The capital of Canada is Ottawa, which is located in the province of Ontario. Canada has 10 provinces and two territories. Each province has a capital city.

Province/Territories	Capital City
Alberta	Edmonton
British Columbia	Victoria
Manitoba	Winnipeg
New Brunswick	Fredericton
Newfoundland	St. John's
Northwest Territories	Yellowknife
Nova Scotia	Halifax
Nunavut	Iqaluit
Ontario	Toronto
Prince Edward Island	Charlottetown
Quebec	Quebec City
Saskatchewan	Regina
Yukon Territory	Whitehorse

Locate each of the provinces and territories on the map on page 37. Place a dot where each capital city is located and write the name of the capital by the dot.

In 1999, the present Northwest Territories was divided into two parts. The western part remains the Northwest Territories. The eastern part is called Nunavut. *Nunavut* is an Inuit word that means "our land." Iqaluit, which is located on Baffin Island, is the capital.

38

Name _____ Date _____

Geographic Regions and Physical Features of Canada

In Canada one finds mountains, lakes, rivers, vast plains, large bays, and islands.

The Canadian Shield

The Canadian Shield is located in parts of Quebec, Manitoba, Ontario, the Northwest Territories, and Nunavut Territory. The Canadian Shield is an area of old mountains that are now worn down and are much lower than they once were. This area is called a shield because the old, hard rock forms a shield area around the Hudson Bay area. This region is very rich in minerals.

As glaciers advanced and retreated across this area, they stripped off all but a thin layer of soil under which are old gneiss and granite rock. The gneiss and granite are igneous rocks. Igneous rocks are formed in areas of volcanic activity. Although these rocks are very old, they do indicate that in the past, the region would have been a mountainous region much like the Rockies of today.

Although not extremely high, the shield is an upland area with many lakes, streams, and large stands of coniferous forests containing spruce, fir, and pine trees. Short rivers flow across the shield from lake to lake and then tumble off the shield to the St. Lawrence Valley. Lumbering and mining are important industries found along many of these short, rapidly flowing rivers. Towns like Sudbury, Ontario; Val d'Or, Quebec; and Flin Flon, Manitoba, are mining towns where zinc, copper, gold, and silver are mined.

Refer to the map on page 44. Shade in the area between the dashed line and the Hudson Bay. This is the area of the Canadian Shield.

Use the terms below to complete the blanks in the following selection.

pine	**St. Lawrence**	**lumber**	**gneiss**	**fir**	**igneous**
glaciers	**Canadian**	**granite**	**spruce**	**mining**	

The (1) _____ Shield is a region of old, worn down mountains. This region was scoured by the action of (2) _____, leaving a layer of thin soil and exposed (3) _____ rock. (4) _____ and (5)_____ are two kinds of rock found here. The (6) _____ industry is very important on the Canadian Shield because large stands of (7) _____ , (8) _____, and (9) _____ trees are found there. The rivers are short and rapidly flowing and tumble off the Canadian Shield to the (10) _____ _____ Valley in the southeast. Along these rivers are many small (11)_____ towns where gold, zinc, and lead are processed.

Name _____ Date _____

12. Choose diagram "a," "b," or "c" below that best describes the rivers as they flow from the Canadian Shield to the St. Lawrence Valley.

a.

b.

c.

Mountains

     Canada has many chains of mountains that add to the beauty of the country. Extending from the United States into New Brunswick and Nova Scotia are the Appalachians. The high rugged Rocky Mountains are found in the west.

     The Rocky Mountains extend north from the United States across Canada to Alaska. Mt. Mackenzie, Mount St. Elias, and the Coast Mountains are all found in western Canada. Mount Logan (6,000 m) is the tallest peak in Canada.

  1. Refer to the map on page 44. Locate Mt. Mackenzie, Mount St. Elias, and Mount Logan. Show the mountains using the following symbol ⋀ . Label each mountain and indicate the height of each.

Lakes

     Canada is a land of many beautiful lakes. Four of the five Great Lakes, Lake Superior, Lake Huron, Lake Erie, and Lake Ontario, are shared with the United States. Great Bear Lake, Great Slave Lake, Lake Athabasca, and Lake Winnipeg are other large lakes that extend in a northwesterly direction from near the city of Winnipeg almost to the border of Alaska. The Great Bear Lake is the largest lake entirely in Canada with an area of 31,326 square kilometers.

  1. Refer to the map on page 44. Color each of the following lakes blue and label them.

Lake Superior	**Lake Huron**	**Lake Erie**	**Lake Ontario**
Great Bear Lake	**Lake Winnipeg**	**Lake Athabasca**	**Great Slave Lake**

Name_____ Date _____

The Great Plains

The following words will appear in the reading selection below. Match each term with the appropriate definition. Use a dictionary if necessary.

_____ 1. plains   A. Source of oil, kerosene, and gas

_____ 2. extension   B. Several or many

_____ 3. petroleum   C. Great in size

_____ 4. various   D. Broad, flat, free from obstacles

_____ 5. vast   E. Part of

_____ 6. endless   F. Going on forever

One of the major geographic regions of Canada is the plains area in Alberta, Saskatchewan, and Manitoba. These plains are an extension of the Great Plains region of the United States. This is one of the world's major grain-producing areas. Wheat and other grains are raised on the plains. The countryside is dotted with grain elevators where the wheat is stored and sold. Winnipeg is an important city from which large amounts of wheat are shipped by rail to the Great Lakes. There the wheat is shipped to various parts of the world. This vast plain goes on for miles and is seemingly endless. This region is also noted for large deposits of natural gas and petroleum. Calgary and Edmonton are cities that have grown rapidly to serve the industry associated with the nearby gas and petroleum fields.

Complete the blanks with one of the following terms or phrases.

Calgary	**stored**	**Winnipeg**	**Edmonton**
wheat	**Canada**	**Great Plains**	**United States**
sold	**ports**	**Alberta**	**Great Lakes**
elevators			

The Great Plains region of (7) _____ includes Alberta, Saskatchewan,

and Manitoba. The plains are an extension of the (8) _____ _____ in the

(9) _____ _____.

The plains region of Canada is a major (10)_____ -producing area of the

world. The grain is taken to (11) _____ where it is (12) _____ and

(13)_____ .

Name _____ Date _____

Three important cities in the region are (14) _____, (15) _____,

and (16) _____ . (17) _____ is a city from which large amounts

of grain are shipped to (18) _____ on the (19) _____ _____

_____ . (20) _____ and (21) _____ are located in

(22) _____ near the petroleum and natural gas fields.

23. Shade in the Great Plains region that is outlined with dashes on the map below.

The Great Lakes Region and St. Lawrence Valley

The Great Lakes and the St. Lawrence Valley region is a special area with a humid continental climate. However, many parts of this area have longer and milder summers than other regions where the humid continental climate is found. As a result, a majority of the population of Canada lives in this area.

The milder climate with a longer growing season than might be expected is a result of the Great Lakes. Large bodies of water, like the Great Lakes, do not heat up as fast in summer nor cool off so much in winter as does land. Therefore, the temperatures for the area nearest the lakes are milder than expected. Summers are longer and more humid than other parts of Canada. Winters often bring heavy snowfall to the region.

The Ontario Peninsula in this region is a very productive farming area. The farms located on the peninsula produce large amounts of oats and hay, which are used to feed the dairy cows found on the large farms. In the region between Lake Ontario and Lake Erie, fruits, such as peaches, grapes, and apples, are grown.

Name _____ Date _____

Refer to the map below and complete the following activity.

1. The Ontario Peninsula is an important farming region. It is particularly noted for dairy farming. Locate and label the Ontario Peninsula.
2. The region between Lake Ontario and Lake Erie is an important fruit-growing region. Locate this area and write peaches, apples, and grapes.
3. Locate and label the St. Lawrence River.
4. Locate and label each of the Great Lakes.
5. A canal and lock system has been developed to allow large ships to come up the St. Lawrence River and into the Great Lakes. The Sault Ste. Marie and Welland locks are two important locks in the system. The Welland locks make it possible for large ships to go from Lake Erie to Lake Ontario. The Sault Ste. Marie locks make it possible for large ships to go from Lake Superior to Lake Huron. Locate and label these locks using the symbol (//////) for the locks.

The Arctic Region

Locate and label the following on the map on page 44.

1. Rocky Mountains
2. Mackenzie River
3. Yukon River
4. Great Slave Lake
5. Great Bear Lake
6. Hudson Bay
7. Baffin Island
8. Victoria Island
9. Queen Elizabeth Islands
10. Ellesmere Island

Name _____ Date _____

Canadian Geography Map

Name _____ Date _____

Canadian Geography Review

Complete the following using the terms below. Some terms may be used for more than one question.

British Columbia   **Alberta**   **Saskatchewan**   **Manitoba**
Ontario   **Quebec**   **Newfoundland**   **New Brunswick**
Prince Edward Island **Nova Scotia**   **Yukon Territory** **Northwest Territories**
Gulf of St. Lawrence **Nunavut Territory**

1. Great Slave Lake is located in the _____ _____ .

2. Great Bear Lake is located in the _____ _____ .

3. Lake Winnipeg is located in the province of _____.

4. The Rocky Mountains are located in the provinces of_____ _____ and
_____ and the_____ and _____ territories.

5. The Appalachian Mountains extend north from the United States into the Canadian
provinces of_____ , _____ _____ , _____
_____ _____ , and _____.

6. The St. Lawrence River forms a boundary between the Canadian province of
_____ and the United States.

7. The St. Lawrence River flows north to empty into the_____ of _____
_____ .

8. The Canadian Shield wraps around the Hudson Bay and is found in the Canadian
provinces of _____, _____ , and _____
and the_____ Territories, and _____ Territory.

9. The Great Plains of Canada are found in the Canadian provinces of _____ ,
_____ , and_____.

Complete the following diagram. Write the term **mountains**, **rivers**, **lakes**, or **islands** on each of the small ovals. Write the name of four Canadian mountains, rivers, lakes, or islands on the lines extending from the appropriate oval.

Name _____ Date _____

Canadian Geography Crossword Puzzle

Use the clues below to complete the crossword puzzle. Refer to the information about Canadian geography on pages 38 through 45 to find the answers.

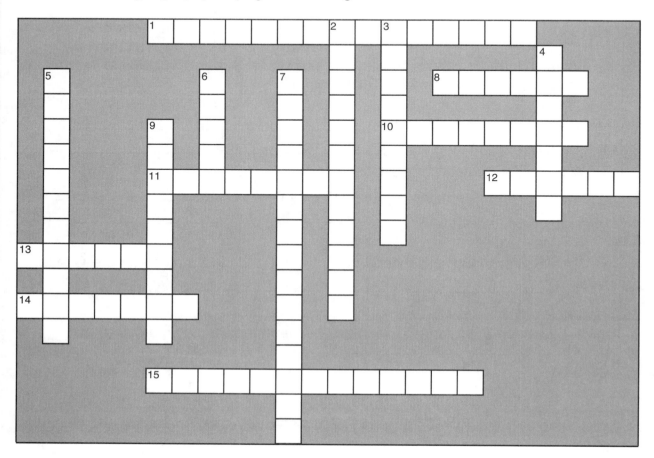

ACROSS

1. River draining the Great Lakes (three words)
8. Large bay named after the explorer of the same name
10. Name of the largest of the Great Lakes
11. Name given to the Rocky Mountains in Canada
12. Capital city of Canada
13. Large island located near Greenland
14. Name of the smallest of the Great Lakes
15. Lake located in the far north of Canada (three words)

DOWN

2. Province that includes an island and the region called Labrador
3. Northernmost Canadian island
4. Capital city of Ontario Province
5. A fertile farming region located in Saskatchewan and Alberta noted for wheat production (two words)
6. Canadian territory bordering Alaska
7. Canadian province that borders Washington State (two words)
9. Canadian river flowing north through the Yukon Territory

    46

Name_____ Date _____

Where Most Canadians Live

Canada has a population of approximately 30 million people. Although a large country in area, Canada has only 0.5 percent of the world's population. Over 75 percent of Canada's people live in cities. The remaining 25 percent live mainly in rural areas. The three largest cities, Toronto, Montreal, and Vancouver, have over one-third of the total population of Canada.

Match the meaning of the term in column A with the definition in Column B.

Column A   **Column B**

_____ 1. Rural   A. Refers to cities

_____ 2. Urban   B. Refers to regions in the country away from cities

Place the following in the appropriate rectangles in the diagram below.

Canada   British Columbia   Ontario   Quebec
Toronto   Vancouver   Montreal

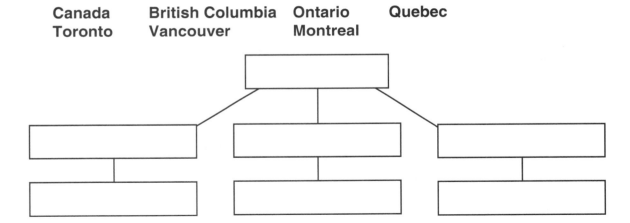

Answer the following questions:

1. The population of Canada is approximately_____ million people.

2. The paragraph above states that 75 percent of Canada's population live in cities. This means that approximately   (a) 25   (b) 18.5   (c) 29   (d) 22.5   million live in cities.

3. The paragraph above states that 25 percent of Canada's population live in rural areas. This means that   (a) 5   (b) 7.5   (c) 9.5   (d) 15   million live in rural areas.

4. The paragraph above states that one-third of Canada's population lives in the cities of Toronto, Vancouver, and Montreal. This means that approximately   (a) 10   (b) 12.5   (c) 8   (d) 13   million of the people in Canada live in Toronto, Vancouver, and Montreal.

Name _____ Date _____

Canada, A Trading Nation

The United States provides the biggest market for Canadian exports. However, Canada trades with nations around the world. With a population of approximately 30 million, Canada is twenty-eighth in population size among the nations of the world. However, Canada is one of the top ten trading nations in the world. Canada's economy is so strong that it is a member of the G-7 nations. The G-7 nations are the seven leading industrialized nations of the world. The G-7 nations include Canada, France, Italy, Germany, Japan, the United Kingdom, and the United States.

Refer to the map below and locate and label each of the G-7 nations.

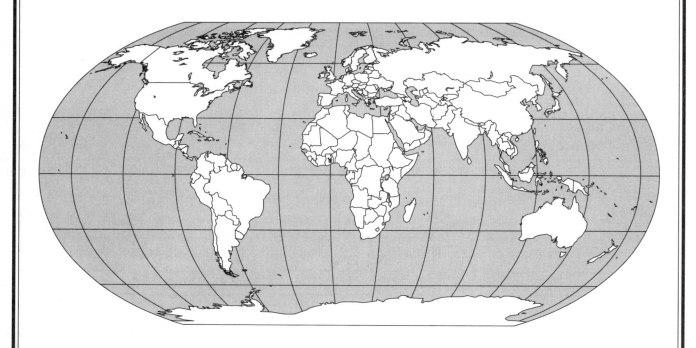

In 1994, Canada, the United States, and Mexico signed an agreement to encourage trade among the three nations. This trade agreement is known as the North American Free Trade Agreement (NAFTA). An important part of the agreement is to lower **tariffs** on goods shipped from one country to another. A tariff is a tax that increases the price that must be paid for a product that is manufactured in one country and sold in another. Over the next few years, Mexico, Canada, and the United States have agreed to lower or end tariffs and allow goods from each country to be sold in the other two countries without tariffs.

Name_____ Date_____

Tariffs and Trade

Here is an example of how tariffs affect trade.

Country A and Country B both make shirts. Country A wants to ship shirts to Country B to be sold. However, Country B wants its people to buy shirts made in Country B. Country B then places a tariff on the shirts from Country A so that the price of a shirt from Country A is higher than the shirts made in Country B.

Read the following, refer to the diagrams, and complete the activity below.

Country A and Country B are neighbors, and they both manufacture radios. The XYZ company in Country A can sell the radio for $25 and make a profit. In Country B, company ABC is producing the same radio, but the ABC company must sell the radio for $30 to make a profit.

ABC company in Country B wants radios produced in Country A and shipped to Country B to be sold at a price higher than $30. People in Country B will then buy the radio made by ABC company because it is the same radio and is cheaper.

ABC company convinces its government to place a tariff on each radio that Country A ships into Country B. ABC company wants the tariff to make the radio from Country A cost more than $30.

Diagram Showing Tariff Placed on Radios From Country A

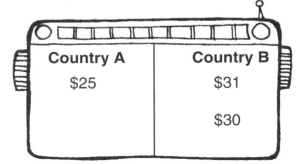

Country A	Country B	
$25	$31	Radio made in Country A
	$30	Radio made in Country B

Refer to the above diagram and answer the following question.

1. You live in Country B. You want to buy a radio. The two radios are the same except one is made in Country A and the other is made in Country B.

Which radio will you buy? _____

Why? _____

_____

Name _____ Date _____

Diagram Showing No Tariff Placed on Radios From Country A

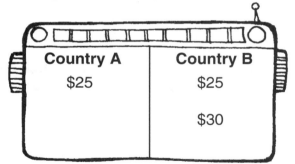

Country A	Country B
$25	$25
	$30

Radio made in Country A

Radio made in Country B

Refer to the above diagram and answer the following question.

2. You live in Country B. You want to buy a radio. The two radios are the same except one is made in Country A and one is made in Country B.

Which radio will you buy? _____

Why? _____

_____

The United States is the biggest buyer of Canada's products. However, nations from around the world, such as Japan, Germany, and Great Britain, are also important trading partners with Canada.

On the map on page 48, locate the United States, Japan, Germany, Great Britain, and Canada. Draw lines with arrows from Canada to each of the other countries. Write the words "exports from Canada" along each of the arrows.

Name _____ Date _____

The Effect of Daylight on Climate

The tilt of the earth on its axis at an angle of $23\frac{1}{2}°$ results in places at higher latitudes having long hours of daylight in summer and long hours of darkness in winter. Canada, which has a large part of its territory located at higher latitudes, has vast areas that have long hours of summer sunlight and long hours of winter darkness. These long periods of daylight and darkness have a very definite effect on the climate. See the diagram below.

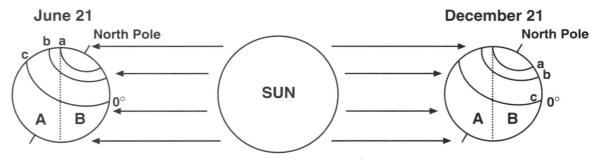

In the diagram above, June 21 is the first day of summer in the Northern Hemisphere, and December 21 is the first day of winter in the Northern Hemisphere. Note how the ray from the Sun strikes the earth at different points on each side of the North Pole. It is important to remember that during the daylight period, a given location is receiving heat from the Sun. During the darkness period, a given location on earth is losing heat.

1. On the diagram above, on June 21, that half of the earth marked (A/B) would have large areas with daylight for that 24-hour period.
2. Shade in that half of the earth that would have a period of darkness on June 21 during the 24-hour period.
3. On the diagram above, on December 21, that half of the earth marked (A/B) would have large areas with daylight for that 24-hour period.
4. Shade in that half of the earth that would have a period of darkness on December 21 during the 24-hour period.

   Assume that individuals are living on the line of latitude marked "a," "b," and "c."

5. On June 21, which individual would have the most hours of darkness in a 24-hour period?

_____

6. On June 21, which individual would have 24 hours of daylight in a 24-hour period?

_____

7. On December 21, which individual would have 24 hours of darkness in a 24-hour period?

_____

Name _____ Date _____

8. On December 21, which individual would have the most hours of daylight in a 24-hour period?

_____

Find a globe and locate Canada and the North Pole. Refer to the diagram on page 51 and answer the following questions.

9. Canada has large areas located near the North Pole. These regions become extremely cold during the winter. On the blanks below, explain why these locations near the North Pole have very cold winter temperatures.

_____

_____

_____

_____

_____

_____

10. Canada has large areas located near the North Pole. These regions become warmer than might be expected during the summer. On the blanks below, explain why these locations near the North Pole have very warm summer temperatures.

_____

_____

_____

_____

_____

_____

Name_____ Date _____

Other Factors Influencing Canada's Climates

Many other factors influence the climates that are found in Canada. The high Rocky Mountains in the west, the location of large parts of the country at a high latitude near the North Pole, the fact that Canada is a large landmass, offshore ocean currents, and the flow of westerly winds all have profound effects on the climates of Canada.

Refer to the map on page 54 and complete the following activity.

1. Label the Pacific Ocean on the map. Use a blue pen, pencil, or crayon to trace over the lines with arrows that are coming from the direction of the polar regions. These lines and arrows represent the ocean current just off the west coast of Canada. This is a cold ocean current. This means that the water in the current is colder than the water it is moving through. The name of this ocean current is the Subarctic Current.

2. Use a red pen, pencil, or crayon to trace over the dashed lines with arrows that are coming from over the Pacific and pointing toward the land. These lines represent the westerly winds that blow from over the ocean toward the western coast of Canada. When these winds blow over the Subarctic Ocean Current, the winds pick up moisture. When the winds come on shore, they begin to rise and drop the moisture. These winds loaded with moisture bring very rainy weather to the western coast of Canada. In the high Canadian Rockies, these winds drop large amounts of snow.

3. Draw the symbol for mountains (/\ /\ ) along the west coast of Canada in British Columbia and the Yukon territory, and along the western borders of Alberta and the Northwest Territories. Label these symbols "Canadian Rockies." These symbols represent the high Canadian Rockies. These high mountains keep the cold winter air over the polar region from reaching the west coast of Canada. When the winds from over the Pacific Ocean rise over the mountains, they drop large amounts of rain and snow. These mountains keep the west coast warmer and wetter than would be normal for this latitude.

4. Complete the following graphic organizer to show five things that cause the types of climates found in Canada. Fill in the rectangles using the terms below.

Westerly Wind Currents   **Canadian Rocky Mountains**
Offshore Ocean Currents   **Large Landmass**
High Latitudes   **Canadian Climates are Affected By:**

Name _____ Date _____

Wind and Ocean Currents Map

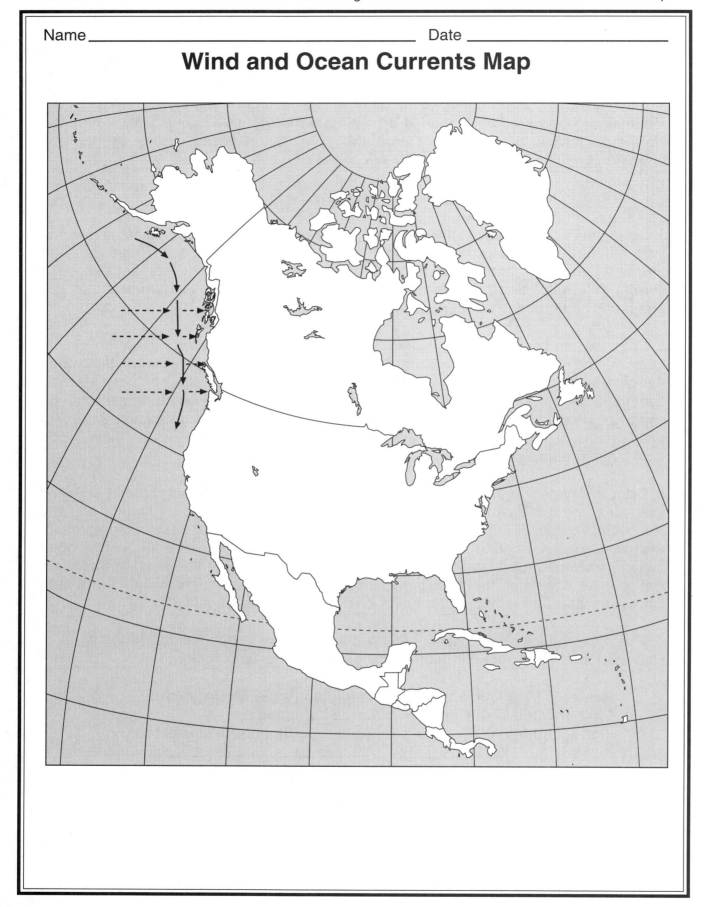

Name _____ Date _____

The Climate Regions of Canada

1. You can see that the Climate Regions Map on page 61 has numbers on it. For each of the numbers on the map, a color is indicated below. Color the map using the color code below. These colors will be used to identify the various climates in Canada.

    1. light green   2. dark green   3. blue   4. yellow   5. purple

Tundra (purple)

This is a region of long, cold winters with snow on the ground for a large part of the year. Summers are short and chilly with at least one month warmer than 32°F. The growing season is very short, and it is too cool for trees to live. However, some mosses, lichens, and grasses grow and bloom here in the short, cool summer. This is a region of **permafrost**. Permafrost refers to the fact that even in summer, the subsoil remains frozen. In the short, cool summer, the top soil layers thaw, but the water cannot drain through the permafrost layer. Therefore, the surface becomes very wet and muddy, making it very difficult for travel.

2. Refer to the Climate Regions Map on page 61. List the Canadian provinces and territories where the tundra climate is found.

_____

_____

Subarctic (blue)

This region has long, bitterly cold winters, with at least one summer month warmer than 50°F. The subarctic region is covered with needle-leaf trees like pines, firs, and spruces. These trees form an evergreen forest that covers the entire region. In the far northern parts of this climate the evergreen trees become shorter as the tundra region is approached. These large northern forested areas with evergreen trees are often referred to as **boreal forests**. This region has large amounts of snowfall that remain on the ground for over half the year. Summers are short, lasting only two months. This is a region where the forest industry is very important. The evergreen trees are cut to make wood pulp and paper. The growing season is only 30 to 90 days.

3. Refer to the Climate Regions Map on page 61. List the Canadian provinces and territories where the subarctic climate is found.

_____

_____

Name _____ Date _____

4. Match the definition in Column B with the appropriate term in Column A.

Column A　　　　　　　　　　　　　**Column B**

_____ Tundra

_____ Subarctic

_____ Boreal

_____ Permafrost

_____ Needle-leaf Trees

A. Found in the tundra region where subsoil remains frozen even in summer

B. Pines, firs, and spruces

C. Climatic area south of the tundra. Region of green forest with long, cold winters and short, cool summers.

D. Climatic area found nearer the polar region. Vegetation consists of mosses, lichen, and grasses. The plants bloom in the short, cool summer. A region of permafrost.

E. Name referring to the evergreen forest found in the subarctic region.

West Coast Marine (light green)

This climate is found along the west coast of Canada. It is a very mild climate with many rainy and cloudy days. This is a region of great forests with large trees, including both evergreen and deciduous trees. The evergreen varieties include trees, like firs and pines, that have needle-leaves. The **deciduous** trees, like oak and maple, have broad leaves that are lost during the winter. The growing season is 150 to 210 days.

This climate is a result of the offshore ocean current, westerly winds, and the high Canadian Rockies. It is a region of **orographic rainfall** in the lower elevations and heavy snowfall in the mountains.

Orographic precipitation occurs when airmasses pick up large amounts of water vapor as they move across a body of water. If the airmass rises, it becomes cooler. The rate at which the airmass cools depends on whether the water is stored as water vapor (a gas form) or if the water vapor has changed to a liquid form as small drops of water. These different cooling temperatures are called **adiabatic lapse rates**.

If you climb a mountain, the temperature will become approximately three degrees cooler for each 1,000-feet increase in altitude. This change in air temperature resulting from the increase in altitude is called the normal lapse rate.

When an airmass moves over a mountain, the airmass cools at the rate of 5.5 degrees for each 1,000-feet increase in altitude. This is known as the **dry adiabatic lapse rate**.

If a mountain is high enough, the airmass will reach a temperature where the water vapor in the airmass changes to little drops of water. Once the water vapor changes to water, the airmass then cools at the rate of 3.3 degrees for each 1,000-feet increase in altitude. This is known as the **wet adiabatic lapse rate**.

Name _____ Date _____

     In the case of the western coast of Canada, the airmass is moving from over the Pacific Ocean where it is like a large sponge picking up water vapor. When the airmass moves on shore and begins to move over the high Canadian Rockies, it is at first cooling at the dry adiabatic lapse rate (5.5° per 1,000 feet).

     Because the airmass is loaded with water vapor it becomes cooler and soon reaches a temperature when the water vapor changes to liquid form as small drops of water. The airmass now begins to cool at the wet adiabatic lapse rate (3.3° per 1,000 feet), and rain or snow will likely fall.

     Airmasses from over the Pacific Ocean move on shore in western Canada and begin to move over the Canadian Rockies (see diagram below). These airmasses are loaded with water vapor, which soon changes to water. Then the water falls as rain or, in many cases, snow in the mountains. Because the airmasses are loaded with water, the west coast of Canada receives 40 to 100 inches of precipitation per year.

     During the winter, very cold masses of air build up over the interior of Canada. Eventually, these large, cold airmasses flow south, bringing very cold weather to southern Canada and the northern United States. However, the Canadian Rockies block the cold air so it cannot enter the west coast area of Canada.

Name _____ Date _____

Semiarid (yellow)

The semiarid or steppe climate is found in the Great Plains area of Canada and the United States. The climate is in the interior of the countries away from the oceans. This climate occurs primarily west of 100°W longitude where the rainfall is 10 to 20 inches per year.

5. Refer to the Climate Regions Map on page 61. List the Canadian provinces where this climate is found.

_____

_____

The high Rocky Mountains are a factor in producing the semiarid climate. These high mountains block the flow of moist air from the Pacific Ocean. In winter, this region often experiences severe winter storms and can experience cold temperatures as large, cold airmasses move south out of the polar regions of Canada. Summers are often very warm, with daytime temperatures often in the 90°F range.

This region in both the United States and Canada was once a grassland area. Although the climate type is semiarid, the term **steppe** is often applied to describe the short grasses that naturally grew in the region. Today, however, large parts of this semiarid region have become important farming areas where grains and livestock are raised. When settlers moved in and established farming, much of the steppe or grassland was destroyed. Grains like wheat, corn, and flax are very important in this region. Large numbers of livestock are also raised.

Winter storms that bring very cold, snowy days are often followed by a warm wind that blows down the Canadian Rockies and across the plains of Alberta, Saskatchewan, and Manitoba. This warm wind brings rapidly rising temperatures and a rapid melting of the snow. The native Americans called this warm wind a **Chinook**. The diagram below illustrates the effects of a Chinook.

Just as an airmass cools when it moves over a mountain, it becomes warmer when it moves down the mountain to lower elevations.

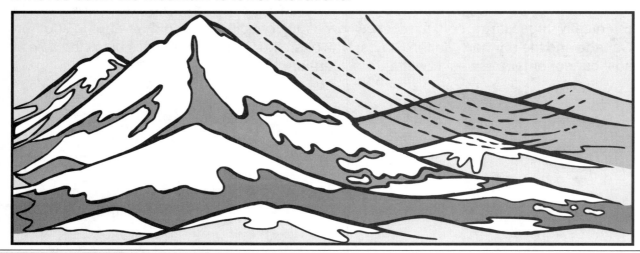

Name _____ Date _____

Refer to the map below and complete the activities that follow.

6. On the map draw in the lines of longitude for 100°W and 115°W.
7. Draw in the line of latitude for 55°N across the provinces of Alberta, Saskatchewan, and Manitoba.
8. The region south of 55°N and between 100°W and 115°W is a large part of the area with a semiarid climate and was the land of natural short grass, or steppe. Color this region yellow.
9. Write the terms "wheat," "corn," "flax," and "livestock" in the yellow-colored area on the map.

10. Match the definition in Column B with the appropriate term in Column A.

Column A

_____ Steppe

_____ Chinook

_____ Semiarid

_____ Orographic

_____ Dry Adiabatic Lapse Rate

_____ West Adiabatic Lapse Rate

Column B

A. Rain or snow produced by an airmass cooling as it rises over a mountain
B. When an airmass moves over a mountain, it cools at the rate of 5.5° per 1,000 feet of altitude until water vapor changes to water or snow
C. Indian name for the warm wind that moves down the slopes of the Rocky Mountains and melts the snow
D. Climate type receiving 10 to 20 inches of rainfall per year, found in Canada in parts of Alberta and Saskatchewan
E. Refers to an airmass that contains drops of water cooling at 3.3° for each 1,000 feet of altitude
F. A vast grassland plains region without trees

Name _____ Date _____

Humid Continental (dark green)

 Summers are cool to warm, with cold winters. Winnipeg, Manitoba, is found in this climatic region. The average temperature for the coldest month is -4°F. The average for the warmest month is 65°F. This climate is marked by weather patterns that change frequently. In winter, cold polar airmasses flow south where they meet warmer and more moist air from over the Gulf of Mexico. The result is often a winter storm that may bring rain, sleet, or snow. In summer, the temperatures are much warmer, and thunderstorms with lightning, heavy rain, or hail may occur. Farming is very important, since there is adequate moisture and the growing season is long enough for crops, like wheat and corn, to mature.

11. On the blanks below, list three Canadian provinces where the humid continental climate is found.

_____

_____

12. List two reasons why farming is important in this climate region.

_____

_____

_____

13. Circle the crops below that might grow in this climate.

  corn   rice   barley   wheat   oranges soybeans

Name _____ Date _____

The Climate Regions of Canada Map

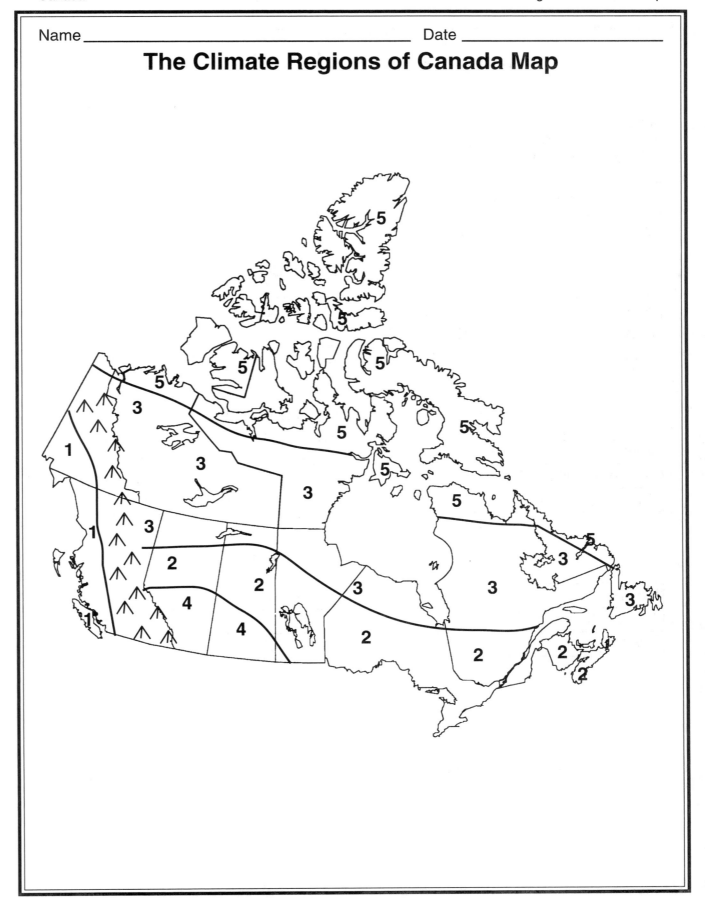

Comparing Canadian Climates

Canada is a nation with extreme climates. Climates range from the very mild west coast marine to the extremely harsh subarctic climates. The climate type found in a particular location in Canada can be greatly influenced by a high latitude location, a large landmass, the high Canadian Rockies, and nearness to the ocean.

Tables I, II, and III below show the average monthly rainfall and temperatures for three climate regions found in Canada. The temperatures shown are Fahrenheit. The rainfall is in inches per month.

Table I: Semiarid/Steppe Climate

Month:	Jan	Feb	Mar	Apr	May	Jun	Jul	Aug	Sep	Oct	Nov	Dec	Year
Temperature:	23	26	38	50	58	64	70	68	58	48	35	28	47
Rainfall:	1.0	0.8	0.3	0.4	0.9	1.2	1.1	1.1	0.8	0.6	1.0	0.9	10.1

Table II: West Coast Marine Climate

Month:	Jan	Feb	Mar	Apr	May	Jun	Jul	Aug	Sep	Oct	Nov	Dec	Year
Temperature:	36	38	42	47	54	59	63	62	56	49	43	48	48
Rainfall:	8.6	6.1	5.3	3.3	3.0	2.7	1.3	1.7	4.1	5.9	10	7.8	59.8

Table III: Subarctic Climate

Month:	Jan	Feb	Mar	Apr	May	Jun	Jul	Aug	Sep	Oct	Nov	Dec	Year
Temperature:	-23	-11	4	29	46	57	59	54	42	25	1	-13	23
Rainfall:	0.8	0.8	0.5	0.7	0.9	1.3	1.6	1.6	1.7	1.3	1.3	1.1	13.6

Name _____ Date _____

Refer to the tables on the previous page and the Climate Regions Map on page 61 and circle the answer that best completes each statement.

1. The climatic type located nearest the North Pole is shown in
    (a) Table I   (b) Table II   (c) Table III.

2. The climatic type located nearest the ocean is shown in
    (a) Table I   (b) Table II   (c) Table III.

3. The climatic type with the greatest difference in average temperature between the warmest and coldest months is shown in   (a) Table I   (b) Table II   (c) Table III.

4. The climatic type with the least difference in average temperature between the warmest and coldest months is shown in   (a) Table I   (b) Table II   (c) Table III.

5. The climatic type with the greatest amount of rainfall per year is shown in
    (a) Table I   (b) Table II   (c) Table III.

6. The climatic type with most of the rainfall coming in the winter months is shown in
    (a) Table I   (b) Table II   (c) Table III.

7. The climatic type with the coldest winter months is shown in
    (a) Table I   (b) Table II   (c) Table III.

8. The climatic type with the warmest temperatures in June, July, and August is shown in
    (a) Table I   (b) Table II   (c) Table III.

9. The climatic type with more rainfall coming in December, January, and February than in June, July, and August is shown in   (a) Table I   (b) Table II   (c) Table III.

10. The climatic type with the lowest average temperature and rainfall for the year is shown in (a) Table I   (b) Table II   (c) Table III.

Arctic Climate Winter

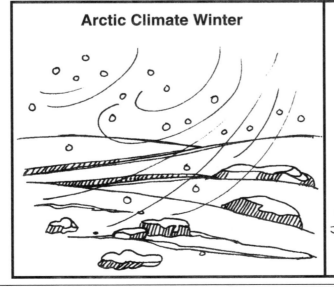

West Coast Marine Climate Winter

Name _____ Date _____

The diagram below shows how the Sun's rays strike the earth at various times throughout the year. The parts of the earth tilted toward the Sun receive more hours of daylight than those areas tilted away from the Sun.

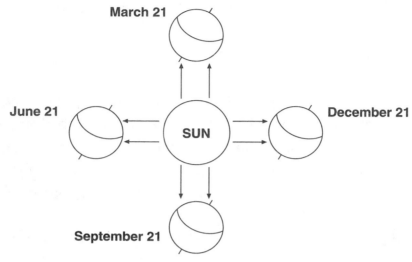

11. Although the subarctic climate is extremely cold, the months of June, July, and August have an average temperature almost as warm as the west coast marine climate. This happens because, as the diagram above shows, the area of Canada with the subarctic climate has a   (shorter/longer)   period of daylight hours during the summer than the west coast marine climate.

12. The subarctic climate is much colder during the months of December, January, and February than is the west coast marine or the semiarid climate. One of the reasons is because, as the diagram above shows, the area of Canada with the subarctic climate has a   (shorter/longer)   period of darkness hours during the winter than the other two climates.

Imagine that it is the middle of winter. The subarctic region is very dark and cold. During this long period of darkness, the airmass over this area becomes very, very cold. Finally, this large, cold airmass begins to move south, bringing extremely cold temperatures to southern Canada. This subarctic airmass brings bitterly cold temperatures to Edmonton, Alberta. However, Vancouver, British Columbia, continues to have mild winter temperatures.

13. On the blanks below, explain why this cold, subarctic airmass that brings such bitter cold to Edmonton, Alberta, does not reach the city of Vancouver, British Columbia.

_____

_____

_____

Name_____ Date _____

Climate Crossword Puzzle

Use the clues below to complete the crossword puzzle. Refer to the information on Canadian climates on pages 55 through 64 to find the answers. You may also use a dictionary if necessary.

ACROSS

2. Treeless plain in arctic regions
4. Refers to the climate region located along the Pacific coast in British Columbia
9. Trees, such as pine, with needle-like leaves that remain on the tree year-round (two words)
10. Fungus-like plant growing in the arctic

DOWN

1. Same as the semiarid climate; region of short grasses receiving 10 to 20 inches of rainfall each year
3. Regions bordering or near the sea
5. Region north of the Arctic Circle
6. Name given to large coniferous forests found in the subarctic climate region of Canada
7. Name given to subsoil that remains fro-zen year-round in the arctic
8. Trees, such as oak and maple, that lose their leaves in winter (two words)

Name _____ Date _____

Latitude and Daylight

The table below shows the approximate number of hours of daylight for each 24-hour period for various latitudes. Listed below are selected Canadian cities with the latitude location for each. Refer to the chart to answer the questions that follow.

Daylight Period in Each 24 Hours

June 21 (first day of summer)		December 21 (first day of winter)	
90°N	24 hours	90°N	0 hours
80°N	24 hours	80°N	0 hours
70°N	24 hours	70°N	0 hours
60°N	18 hours	60°N	6 hours
50°N	16 hours	50°N	8 hours
40°N	15 hours	40°N	9 hours

Yellowknife 62°N   Calgary 52°N   Quebec 45°N
Winnipeg 50°N   Whitehorse 61°N

1. Approximately how many hours of daylight in December at Whitehorse? _____

2. Approximately how many hours of daylight in June at Whitehorse? _____

3. Approximately how many hours of daylight in December at Yellowknife? _____

4. Approximately how many hours of daylight in June at Yellowknife? _____

5. Approximately how many hours of daylight in December at Calgary? _____

6. Approximately how many hours of daylight in June at Calgary? _____

7. Approximately how many hours of daylight in December at Winnipeg? _____

8. Approximately how many hours of daylight in June at Winnipeg? _____

9. Approximately how many hours of daylight in December at Quebec? _____

10. Approximately how many hours of daylight in December at Quebec? _____

11. The two cities closest to the North Pole are _____ and _____.

12. The cities with the greatest difference in hours of daylight from December to June are

_____ and _____ .

13. The cities with the least difference in hours of daylight from December to June are

_____ and _____ .

Name _____ Date _____

Based on what is observed about the length of daylight hours from December to June, answer the following questions.

14. The closer a location is to the North Pole, the (smaller/greater) the amount of daylight

in the summer.

15. The closer a location is to the North Pole, the (smaller/greater) the amount of daylight

in the winter.

16. Based on what has been observed about the difference in hours of daylight for the above locations, arrange the following U.S. and Canadian cities in order from smallest to greatest difference in hours of daylight from December to June.

City	Latitude	Smallest to Greatest Difference in Daylight
Whitehorse	61°N	_____
New Orleans	30°N	_____
St. Louis	38°N	_____
Minneapolis	45°N	_____
Winnipeg	50°N	_____
Yellowknife	62°N	_____

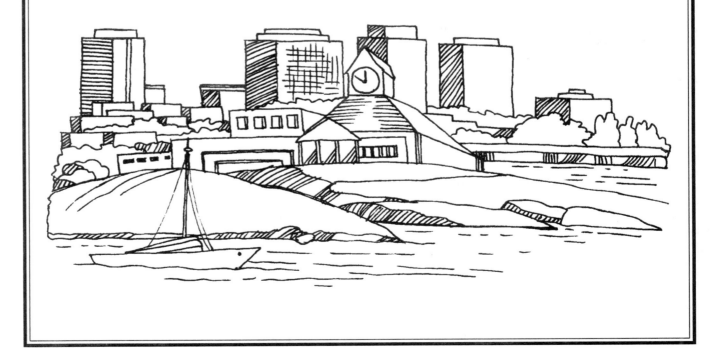

Name _____ Date _____

Planning Activities With
Latitude and Daylight Hours in Mind

Refer to a globe or Canadian map and locate Victoria Island, Great Bear Lake, and Baffin Island. Also refer to the daylight chart on page 66 to answer the following questions.

1. The line of latitude that crosses Victoria Island is   (a) 40°N   (b) 50°N   (c) 60°N
   (d) 70°N.

2. The line of latitude that crosses Great Bear Lake is   (a) 50°N   (b) 55°N   (c) 65°N
   (d) 70°N.

3. The line of latitude that crosses Baffin Island is   (a) 40°N   (b) 50°N   (c) 60°N
   (d) 70°N.

4. You and a friend have the opportunity to go to Victoria Island on a sightseeing trip. You must choose to be on the island in June or December. On the blanks below, tell which month you would choose and why.

_____

_____

_____

5. A friend tells you he/she can go on a fishing trip to Great Bear Lake. The friend asks you what months you would suggest for the trip. On the blanks below, write the months you suggest and explain why you chose those months.

_____

_____

_____

6. You are in Whitehorse on a winter vacation. It is during the month of December. Many of the activities that are planned must occur when there is daylight. Approximately how many hours of daylight will you have for these activities? _____

7. You are in Whitehorse on a summer vacation. It is during the month of June. Many of the activities that are planned must occur when there is daylight. Approximately how many hours of daylight will you have for these activities? _____

Name _____ Date _____

8. In December, if you travel from Calgary to Yellowknife, the amount of daylight in a 24-hour period will be   (a) 1 hour   (b) 4 hours   (c) 2 hours   (d) 10 hours   less in Yellowknife.

Each degree of latitude equals approximately 69 miles. Answer the following questions.

9. The distance from Calgary to Whitehorse in degrees is   (a) 9   (b) 40   (c) 5   (d) 3.

10. The distance, in miles, from Calgary to Whitehorse is approximately   (a) 90   (b) 457   (c) 621   (d) 1,240.

You will need a globe or world map for the following questions.

11. A large part of Canada is located north of 50°N latitude. Refer to a globe or map and tell which of the following countries have a large part of their territory located north of 50°N latitude. (Circle all answers that apply).

| Russia | China | Brazil | Great Britain | Sweden |
| India | Australia | Spain | Norway | |

12. Russia, Canada, and Great Britain all have a large part of their territory located north of 50°N latitude. Russia and Canada have large areas that experience very cold winters. Even though Great Britain is located at the same latitude, it has a much milder climate. Place a plus sign (+) by those statements that might explain why the climate is much colder in Canada and Russia.

_____ a. Great Britain is a smaller landmass.

_____ b. Great Britain is located much closer to the equator than is any part of Canada or Russia.

_____ c. Great Britain is surround by a large body of water with a warm ocean current nearby.

_____ d. Climate type is not affected by latitude location of a country, so having similar latitudes does not affect climate.

_____ e. Canada and Russia have large landmasses that cool off rapidly in winter.

_____ f. Warm winds from off the ocean do not reach the interiors of Canada or Russia.

_____ g. All three countries have capitals with a population over one million.

_____ h. Canada and Russia are on the polar sides of large continental landmasses.

Name _____ Date _____

Canadian Sports

Winter Sports

Canadians are very active people who enjoy sports. Because the country has winters with cold temperatures and lots of snowfall, winter is a time of great sports activity.

Winter sports include figure and speed skating for which Canadians are recognized worldwide. Canadians often capture medals when competing internationally in these sports.

A new sport that many female Canadians participate in is Ringette. This sport is played much like ice hockey except it uses a rubber ring instead of the puck used in regular hockey. Ringette has become very popular, and teams from across Canada have been formed and engage in scheduled play.

Another winter sport that has excited many Canadians is the Biathlon. This very strenuous sport involves cross country skiing and shooting.

Hockey

Of course, hockey is the sport that has long been identified with Canada. Professional hockey has a long history in Canada. Eight of the 26 teams that comprise the National Hockey League are located in Canadian cities. Each year the National Hockey League season concludes with playoffs. The winner of the playoffs receives the Stanley Cup and is declared to be the league champion.

Hockey is also played by thousands of young people. Almost all communities in Canada have hockey teams that engage in league competition. Many of these young people become stars in the National Hockey League.

Refer to the sports page of a major newspaper or another source and identify the name given to the National Hockey League team found in each of the following Canadian cities. Write the team name on the blank next to the city.

NHL City	Team Name
1. Calgary	_____
2. Edmonton	_____
3. Montreal	_____
4. Ottawa	_____
5. Quebec	_____
6. Toronto	_____
7. Vancouver	_____
8. Winnipeg	_____

Name _____ Date _____

Summer and Fall Sports

Football

The most popular summer/fall sport in Canada is football. The Canadian Football League (CFL) is a professional league. The equipment worn by the players is much like that worn by professional football players in the United States. However, the rules for playing are different.

The CFL season begins in the middle of June and ends in late November with the Grey Cup Game. This game is one of the year's most important sporting events. It is watched by millions of Canadians.

Each of the following Canadian cities has a team in the CFL. Place a dot to locate each of the cities on the map below. Write the name of the team by the dot that locates the city.

Western Division

British Columbia Lions (Vancouver)
Calgary Stampeders
Edmonton Eskimos
Saskatchewan Roughriders (Regina)
Winnipeg Blue Bombers

Eastern Division

Hamilton Tiger-Cats
Montreal Alouettes
Ottawa Rough Riders
Toronto Argonauts

Name _____ Date _____

Baseball

Canada is the only nation outside of the United States that hosts National League and American League baseball. In 1992 and 1993, Toronto won the World Series. This was the first time the World Series had been won by a team that was not located in the United States.

Refer to maps, newspapers, or other sources. Place each of the following terms under the city associated with that term.

**Blue Jays   American League   Ontario   Quebec
National League   Expos   Won World Series in 1992/93**

Montreal   **Toronto**

_____   _____

_____   _____

_____   _____

_____   _____

Answer Keys

Exploration and Settlement of Canada (pages 1–2)
1, 3, 4. Teacher check map work.
2. Henry Hudson
5. Jacques Cartier
6. English
7. French
8. Samuel de Champlain

The French and English in Canada (pages 3–4)
1–5. Teacher check map work.
Matching (page)
6. C, 7. B, 8. A, 9. D, 10. G, 11. E

Canadian Time Line (page 4)
1. Aboriginal peoples migrate to Canada from Asia.
2. Lief Ericson explores Newfoundland and Atlantic Coast of Canada.
3. Jacques Cartier explores Gulf of St. Lawrence and St. Lawrence River.
4. Samuel de Champlain explores the St. Lawrence and Great Lakes.
5. Henry Hudson explores Hudson Bay region.

Aboriginal Inhabitants of Canada (page 5)
Matching
1. C, 2. D, 3. A, 4. B
Teacher check map work.
5. c
6. a
7. Arctic, Bering Strait

First Nations (page 6)
2, 1, 5, 3, 4

Inuits, A First Nation (pages 7–8)
The following statements should be marked with a plus sign: 1, 3, 5, 6, 8.
Teacher check map work.

Inuit Crossword Puzzle (page 9)

War Develops Between France and England (page 10)
1. British Colony
2. 1756
3. Treaty of Paris
4. French and Indian
5. French

6. Quebec
7. New France
8. Quebec Act

Canada Becomes Home to the Loyalists (page 11)
1–3. Teacher check map work.

Canada Becomes a Constitutional Monarchy (page 12)
1. E, 2. B, 3. C, 4. D, 5. A
6. A, 7. B, 8. E, 9. D, 10. C

Canada and Its Neighbor to the South Expand West-ward (pages 13–17)
1. Canadian Time Line
1867 Dominion of Canada
1870 Purchases Hudson Bay and Rupert's Land area
1870 Northwest Territories established
1870 Manitoba becomes province
1871 British Columbia becomes province
1873 Prince Edward Island becomes province
1898 Yukon Territory established
1905 Alberta becomes province
1905 Saskatchewan becomes province
1949 Newfoundland becomes province
1999 Nunavut becomes a territory

2. U.S. Time Line
1783 Original territory gained from England in Revolution-ary War
1803 Louisiana Purchase
1819 Florida annexed
1845 Texas annexed
1846 Oregon Country annexed
1848 Mexican Cession
1853 Gadsden Purchase
1867 Alaska purchased
1898 Hawaii annexed

3–4. Teacher check.
5–6. Teacher check map work.

Canada Becomes an Independent Nation (page 18)
1–2. Teacher check dates. They will vary as time passes.
3. b
4. Teacher check flag.

Canada's Government (page 19)

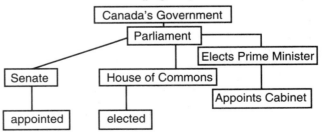

The United States Government (pages 20–21)
1. legislative
2. Congress
3. Senate
4. House of Representatives
5. six
6. two
7. president
8. four
9. cabinet
10. Senate
11. federal
12. national
13. state
14. Teacher check.
15.
A: 1, 7, 9, 10, 12
B: 2, 3, 4, 5, 8,
C: 6, 11

Canada: A Nation of Many Cultures (page 22)
Teacher check map work.

The French Acadians Leave Nova Scotia (page 24)
1–3. Teacher check map work.

The French Acadians in Longfellow's "Evangeline" (pages 25–26)
1. Teacher check.
2. B, G, I, C, H, A, D, J, E, F
3–4. Teacher check.

The Atlantic Provinces (page 27)
1. Prince Edward Island
2. Nova Scotia, New Brunswick
3. Newfoundland
4. Newfoundland
5. Nova Scotia
6. Prince Edward Island
7. New Brunswick
8. b

The Unique Bay of Fundy (pages 28–29)
1. Teacher check.
2. b
3. b
4. a
5. d
6–7. Teacher check.
8. b
9. b
10. c
11. a
12. Moon
13. The gravitational effect of the Moon attracts water toward the Moon. It also pulls the earth toward the Moon, so water on the opposite side of the earth bulges at high tide.
14. b
15. b

Quebec (page 30)
1–2. Teacher check map work.

Canada's Population
Population Growth (page 31)

1998	30,000,000	1.0	30,300,000
1999	30,300,000	1.0	30,603,000
2000	30,603,000	1.0	30,909,030
2001	30,909,030	1.0	31,218,120
2002	31,218,120	1.0	31,530,301
2003	31,530,301	1.0	31,845,604
2004	31,845,604	1.0	32,164,060
2005	32,164,060	1.0	32,485,700
2006	32,485,700	1.0	32,810,557
2007	32,810,557	1.0	33,138,662

Comparing Canada to Other Nations of the World
Area (page 32)
1. Russia
2. Canada
3. China
4. United States
5. Brazil
6. Australia
7. India
8. Argentina
9. Kazakstan
10. Algeria

Graph I
Teacher check graph.

Population (page 33)
1. China
2. India
3. United States
4. Indonesia
5. Brazil
6. Russia
7. Pakistan
8. Japan
9. Bangladesh
10. Mexico

Graph II
Teacher check graph.

Finding the Number of Persons Per Square Mile (page 34)
1. 23
2. 331
3. 49
4. 73
5. 743
6. 8

Finding the Ratio of Canadians to Other Nations of the World (page 35)
1a. 5, b. 5/1
2a. 5, b. 5/1
3a. 9, b. 9/1
4a. 31, b. 31/1
5a. 40, b. 40/1

Where Canada's Population Lives (pages 36–37)
1–2. Teacher check map work.
4. b
5. All statements should be marked with a plus sign.

Provinces and Territories (page 38)
Teacher check map work.

**Geographic Regions and Physical Features of Canada
The Canadian Shield (pages 39–40)**
1. Canadian
2. glaciers
3. igneous
4. gneiss
5. granite
6. lumber
7, 8, 9. spruce/pine/fir
10. St. Lawrence
11. mining

12. a

Mountains (page 40)
1. Teacher check map work.

Lakes (page 40)
1. Teacher check map work.

The Great Plains (pages 41–42)
1. D, 2. E, 3. A, 4. B, 5. C, 6. F

7. Canada
8. Great Plains
9. United States
10. wheat
11. elevators
12. stored
13. sold
14, 15, 16. Winnipeg/Edmonton/Calgary
17. Winnipeg
18. ports
19. Great Lakes
20, 21. Edmonton/Calgary
22. Alberta
Teacher check map work.

Great Lakes Region and St. Lawrence Valley (pages 42–43)
Teacher check map work.

The Arctic Region (page 43)
Teacher check map work.

Canadian Geography Review (page 45)
1. Northwest Territories
2. Northwest Territories
3. Manitoba
4. British Columbia, Alberta, Yukon, Northwest
5. Quebec, New Brunswick, Prince Edward Island, Newfoundland
6. Ontario
7. Gulf of St. Lawrence
8. Quebec, Ontario, Manitoba, Northwest, Nunavut
9. Alberta, Saskatchewan, Manitoba
Teacher check diagram.

Canadian Geography Crossword Puzzle (page 46)

Where Most Canadians Live (page 47)
1. B, 2. A

1. 30
2. d
3. b
4. a

Canada, A Trading Nation (page 48)
Teacher check map work.

Tariffs and Trade (pages 49–50)
1. The radio made in Country B.
The radio from Country B costs less.
2. The radio made in Country A.
The radio from Country A costs less.

Teacher check map work.

The Effect of Daylight on Climate (pages 51–52)
1. B
2. Shade A
3. A
4. Shade B
5. c

75

6. a
7. a
8. c
9. There are short periods of daylight and long, winter nights.
10. They have long periods of daylight with short nighttime periods.

Other Factors Influencing Canada's Climates (pages 53–54)
1–3. Teacher check map work.
4.

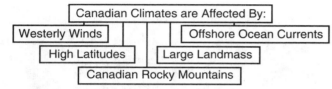

Canadian Climates are Affected By:
Westerly Winds | Offshore Ocean Currents
High Latitudes | Large Landmass
Canadian Rocky Mountains

The Climate Regions of Canada (page 55)
1. Teacher check map work.
Tundra (page 55)
2. Yukon Territories, Northwest Territories, Nunavut Territory, Quebec, Newfoundland
Subarctic (pages 55–56)
3. Yukon Territories, Northwest Territories, Nunavut Territory, British Columbia, Alberta, Saskatchewan, Manitoba, Ontario, Quebec, Newfoundland
4. D, C, E, A, B
Semiarid (pages 58–59)
5. British Columbia, Alberta, Saskatchewan, Manitoba
6–9. Teacher check map work.
10. F, C, D, A, B, E
Humid Continental (page 60)
11. British Columbia, Alberta, Saskatchewan, Manitoba, Ontario, Quebec, New Brunswick, Prince Edward Island,
Nova Scotia (any three)
12. There is adequate moisture and a long growing season.
13. corn, barley, wheat

Comparing Canadian Climates (pages 62–64)
1. c, 2. b, 3. c, 4. b, 5. b, 6. b, 7. c, 8. a, 9. b, 10. c
11. longer, 12. shorter
13. The high Canadian Rockies block out the cold air masses.

Climate Crossword Puzzle (page 65)

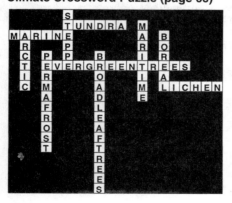

Latitude and Daylight (pages 66–67)
1. 6   2. 18   3. 6   4. 18   5. 8
6. 16   7. 8   8. 16   9. 8–9   10. 15–16
11. Yellowknife, Whitehorse
12. Yellowknife, Whitehorse
13. Winnipeg, Quebec
14. greater
15. less
16. New Orleans
St. Louis
Minneapolis
Winnipeg
Whitehorse
Yellowknife

Planning Activities With Latitude and Daylight Hours in Mind (pages 68–69)
1. d, 2. c, 3. d
4. June; There are long daylight hours.
5. The summer months: There are long daylight hours.
6. 6, 7. 18, 8. c, 9. a, 10. c
11. Russia, Great Britain, Sweden, Norway
12. The following statements should be marked with a plus sign: a, c, e, f, h.

Canadian Sports
Hockey (page 70)
1. Flames
2. Oilers
3. Canadiens
4. Senators
5. Nordiques
6. Maple Leafs
7. Canucks
8. Jets

Football (page 71)
Teacher check map work.

Baseball (page 72)

Montreal	Toronto
Expos	Blue Jays
Quebec	Ontario
National League	American League
	Won World Series in 1992/93